WHEN NIGHT EATS THE MOON

JOANNE FINDON

Red Deer Press

Northern Lights Young Novels are published by
Red Deer Press
56 Avenue & 32 Street Box 5005
Red Deer Alberta Canada T4N 5H5

Credits
Cover art by Igor Kordey
Cover design by Duncan Campbell
Text design by Dennis Johnson
Printed and bound in Canada by Friesens for Red Deer Press

Acknowledgements
Financial support provided by the Canada Council, the Department of Canadian Heritage and the Alberta Foundation for the Arts, a beneficiary of the Lottery Fund of the Government of Alberta.

Author's Acknowledgements
I am grateful to the Ontario Arts Council for a small grant that enabled me to revisit Stonehenge and finish an important stage of the rewriting of this book.

This story has had a long and difficult birth. To those who helped it along, especially my wonderful friends in the Writing for Children workshops in Toronto who listened patiently to draft upon draft and wondered if Holly would *ever* find her way, a hearty, heartfelt thank-you.

Canadian Cataloguing in Publication Data
Findon, Joanne, 1957–
When night eats the moon
(Northern lights young novels)
ISBN 0-88995-212-4
I. Title. II. Series.
PS8561.I5387   1999   jC813'.54   C99-910348-2
PZ7.F56Wh 1999

5   4   3   2   1

Sasha Taylor
xox

Contents

For Steve, with love

THE DREAM

"THE FLUTE SHE HAS IS JUST FINE—"

"No, it's not—the tone isn't there. She needs a professional model now."

Holly floated on the edge of the muffled voices, caught between them and her dream. It was *that* dream again.

"Dare I ask how much we'll be throwing away?"

"Burton's has a used Hanes for three thousand dollars."

"Three thou—!"

"Shhh!"

In the dream, there were mountains all around her, black and jagged as broken teeth. These mountains were shadowed somehow, as if the sun had just gone behind a cloud or as if she were looking at an old, stained photograph.

"Too much! Besides, this music thing is getting out of hand."

"Out of hand? Have you bothered to notice that she loves it? And she's good, really good—"

"Wake up, David. How many people make it as musicians—I mean, really make it? One in ten thousand."

"More than that. . . ."

"She'll only be disappointed."

If the dream lasted long enough, she would climb up a rocky path and struggle through the prickly, fragrant branches of hemlocks to another place, a place just as strange, a place of rolling hills and bright, threadlike streams. This place was in black and white too, but colour seemed to tremble just beneath its surface, as if she might suddenly call it forth by . . . by doing what? She couldn't tell.

"What if she succeeds?"

"What are the chances? Look at you, after all these years of dreaming."

Holly slipped out of bed and drew the curtain aside. Outside, above the glow of the streets below, the lights of the ski lift on Grouse Mountain looped themselves like a necklace across the black sky.

The dream still tugged at her.

"Holly's different. I never had the drive she has. Besides, money isn't everything. . . ."

"So you keep saying. The bottom line is that Holly's going to need marketable skills. I don't want her busking on street corners for the rest of her life. . . ."

Holly slid back into bed and tried to shut the voices out. As sleep pulled her back in, the voices faded and she thought she heard the faint sound of a flute, high and wild, echoing through mountain passes and calling her to some other country.

CHAPTER ONE
STONEHENGE

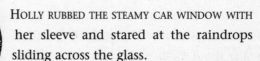

HOLLY RUBBED THE STEAMY CAR WINDOW WITH her sleeve and stared at the raindrops sliding across the glass.

"Almost there!" said Aunt Sally over her shoulder.

Mum sat up straighter beside her and tried to peer outside.

Holly's heartbeat quickened. Stonehenge! For years she had longed to come here and walk among these stones, to run her hand along their cool sides and stand in their shadows. All those hours spent with Dad, bent over countless books and photographs—Stonehenge at dawn, Stonehenge against a stormy sky. . . .

The car and the rain and the flapping wipers slid away. In her mind she was Holly, high priestess of the sun god, leading her people to Stonehenge for the yearly sacrifice. She stepped into the middle of the circle while the respectful crowd halted and waited. The tall stones enclosed her with their power, and she was alone. As she raised her arms to the sun, her crimson robes billowed around her. *Crimson*—she loved that word. Okay, so Dad would say these people wouldn't have had crimson robes because they had no red dye; but this was *her* fantasy.

Her stomach knotted suddenly as the vision slipped away. Dad. He should be here with her; they should be seeing Stonehenge together.

"There it is, Holly!" Mum pointed out the window. Holly could only make out a grey blur as Aunt Sally turned off the main road and into a parking lot.

"Filthy weather!" grumbled Frederick, Aunt Sally's son. He was about Holly's age, but he might as well have been from another planet for all they had in common.

"Right!" said Aunt Sally briskly, pulling on the parking brake. "Out you get, Frederick. The brollies are in the boot."

Holly climbed stiffly out and pulled up the hood of her yellow rain jacket. It was still pouring rain. It had rained every single day since they'd arrived in England ten days ago. And it would probably rain every single day after Mum left for her holiday with Dad, a holiday that didn't include Holly. She had to stay with Aunt Sally and Uncle Ian and grumpy old Frederick, here in soggy England. Three weeks, Mum said. Holly let the pounding of the rain on the car roof drown out that thought.

She watched Aunt Sally bustling about, opening the trunk and taking out their umbrellas. After a fierce struggle against the wind, Holly managed to open the big black umbrella that was handed to her. She pushed the wet bangs away from her eyes and looked around.

Beyond where Aunt Sally had parked the car, several huge buses were disgorging crowds of noisy tourists in bright rain gear. They milled about in tight groups, snapping purses, opening umbrellas, rustling damp maps.

"Right," said Aunt Sally. "In we go. This is my treat, now." She pulled out a handful of coins.

"What . . . you mean we have to *pay?*" asked Holly in horror as they followed the crowd of tourists.

"Afraid so, love," grimaced Aunt Sally. "The place has to be kept up, doesn't it?"

"But . . ." Holly stopped still as the crowded turnstile came into view in front of them; across from it, an open window sold snacks and coffee to a line of hungry visitors. As she tipped her umbrella back in dismay, she finally saw the stones.

They stood across the road behind a wire fence, dark, looming shapes huddled together in the mist. Holly knew the stones from photos and paintings, but here they seemed smaller than she had expected, like captives behind bars. A line of people stood around them in a crescent, desperately snapping pictures beneath their umbrellas. A couple of men even had video cameras, although it didn't seem like the stones were about to get up and walk off. A low rope barrier kept everyone well away from the monument. As Holly gazed at the scene, the air was shattered by the boom of an invisible jet.

"I can't go in here!" cried Holly, taking a step backwards. "It's horrible! Mum, why didn't you tell me?"

Mum's hand gripped her shoulder. "Holly," she said, "I'm so sorry. It wasn't like this the last time I was here."

Holly's throat was tight with rage. "How could they do this?"

"You can still see them," muttered Frederick, eyeing Holly warily.

And he was right. The giant stones stood there on their hilltop, lashed by wind and rain, still brooding and powerful. But their power was leashed, controlled.

Holly choked back the tears. "Why did they have to do this? You can't get close at all!"

"They're just a bunch of old rocks, after all, aren't they?" mumbled Frederick.

Holly glared at him.

"They had to do this, love," said Aunt Sally. "All the people touching them and tramping round them was wearing them away. In the old days, people even used to chip away bits of them for souvenirs. By charging money to see them and fencing them off, the authorities can be sure they're kept safe."

"Safe!" cried Holly. "They're ruined!"

"Well, they are ruins, aren't they?" said Frederick.

Holly snapped her umbrella closed and ran back towards the car. For a brief instant the sting of the rain on her face allowed her to imagine she ran alone and free, like the people who had built Stonehenge. She could almost feel those crimson robes whispering around her legs as she ran, but the reek of diesel fuel from the buses closed around her, and the fantasy dissolved in tatters.

She half-expected the others to go in without her, but they didn't. In a few moments everyone was back in the car, damp and quiet and tense. Holly chewed the side of one fingernail and glared out the window as Aunt Sally pulled the car around and out of the parking lot.

Everything just kept getting worse and worse. Holly blinked back tears as the memory crashed down on her like a wall of cold water.

How many times had she relived those few seconds?

Dad standing at the sink draining pasta, looking carefully down at the shiny noodles through the steam rising around his face.

"You'll have to give my regards to the old stones," he said in a quiet, tight voice.

"What?" Holly dropped the cutlery on the counter and faced him.

"I'm not coming, Holly. Not this time."

"Not coming!" She gaped at him. "Why?"

"We—your mum and I—we need some time away from each

*other and . . . and Mum needs to spend some time with her sister,
now that Granddad's gone."*

*"And what about me?" Holly demanded. "What about what I
need?"*

"I'm sorry, Piper, I didn't know how to tell you. . . ."

*And he turned away from her, back to the steaming noodles, his
shoulders hunched and unreadable.*

The memory of that moment still stung. How could Dad
turn away? How could he let her go to England without him?
And what had he meant about him and Mum needing time
away from each other? The worst thing was, she couldn't *do*
anything about it. Dad was thousands of miles away, and
Mum didn't seem to want to talk about him.

As for England . . . well, England had been one disappoint-
ment after another. First the airline had lost her luggage for
three days, and then all the shows she and Mum had wanted
to see in London were either sold out or too expensive. And
since they'd come here, the constant rain had kept them
cooped up in this tiny old farmhouse, away from all the his-
toric places that Holly wanted to see. Mum seemed on edge all
the time, Aunt Sally was terminally cheerful, and Frederick's
sullen grouchiness grated on her like the buzzing of a fly
against a window. Everything was getting on her nerves.

Holly sank down in the back seat, trying to make herself
small.

Oh, Dad! Why couldn't you be here?

CHAPTER TWO
POTS

AUNT SALLY'S KITCHEN GLOWED. WITH ITS peach walls, flowered curtains, and stout, potted plants on the windowsill, it looked like something out of a Beatrix Potter book. Holly felt a little better as she ate her second helping of something that Aunt Sally called pudding. It was really a thick piece of cake with hot custard sauce poured over it.

"Those Portuguese fish were amazing! Long as your right arm!" Uncle Ian was leaning back in his chair, puffing on his pipe, while Mum stirred her tea and smiled.

"Don't let him get away with his fish stories, Gillian!" Aunt Sally chuckled.

Although they were family, Aunt Sally and Uncle Ian were like strangers to Holly. Mum had left England long ago, and they hadn't visited back and forth much. Granny and Granddad had come to Vancouver a few times, and there was one picture at home of Holly and Frederick together when they were both toddlers. But Holly couldn't remember that visit. After Granny died, Uncle Ian had had a number of jobs overseas fixing heavy machinery, and they'd lived in Greece and then Portugal for a while. But now Granddad was gone, and he'd left the farm to Aunt Sally, and they had come back here to stay last year.

Holly looked sideways at Frederick as she shoveled the last spoonful of pudding into her mouth. He was gripping his spoon and scowling. That baby picture back home showed him clutching a plastic truck and scowling at the camera. Not much had changed.

"There's a film on telly tonight," Aunt Sally said as she cleared away the dishes. "All about Britain in the old days. You'd like it, Holly." She shot Holly a freckled grin.

Holly looked away and pushed back her chair. "Can I practise first?"

"Oh well, of course, love. Go right ahead."

"Um . . . by the way," Holly said as a thought struck her, "could I maybe practise in the barn?"

Aunt Sally looked up in surprise. "Why, of course you can. I'm sure old Emily won't mind."

"I don't think the barn is a good place for you, Holly," said Mum shortly. "It's dirty and cramped, and the air is stifling in there."

"I'll leave the door open," promised Holly. "And it's only for a few minutes."

Now Mum was scowling too. "Well, just stay in the front of the barn then, near Emily. I don't want you poking around in the old part—it's in such disrepair."

"I won't, I promise."

Holly got up and hurried off to the spare room before Mum could change her mind.

She closed the door and rummaged through her music bag. The blue case of her new flute beckoned, and she paused. *Not tonight*, she told herself firmly and pulled out her recorder instead.

Her eyes fell on the book she'd brought with her, the one about ancient Britain that Dad had given her last Christmas. It was filled with pictures of stone circles and lots of information about Stonehenge. Holly sighed, remembering. She and Dad had spent the whole afternoon looking through it and talking about the people who had built Stonehenge. She sank down on the bed and flipped through it. Life must have been simple back then, she thought. People were probably so busy hunting and farming that they never had time to fight.

Mum walked in and pushed the oak door shut behind her. She sat down on the bed opposite.

"Holly, I know you've been upset today, but that's no excuse for bad manners." Her voice was low and taut.

"What did I do now?" demanded Holly.

"Well, aside from your incredible rudeness at Stonehenge this afternoon, you just left the table without even offering to help with the dishes. Really, Holly, I sometimes don't know what to do with you."

Holly glared at the floorboards. "I forgot about the dishes. Sorry."

"Well, try not to forget next time. And I hope I can count on you to apologize to Aunt Sally for that scene in the parking lot. I won't be here much longer to remind you about these things."

"Don't I know it!" Holly couldn't keep the snarl out of her voice. "You'll probably leave me here forever and forget all about me!"

"Holly! What nonsense! We've been through all this before. I only meant—"

"I don't care what you meant. I'm going to practise."

Holly grabbed her recorder and stood up. She flung the door open and stomped down the back hall to the outside door.

It had stopped raining, but the grass in the yard was wet, and Holly almost slipped in her angry haste to be away from the house. Heavy clouds brooded over the yard. Dusk was settling in early.

The garage door yawned open like a golden mouth. Frederick was in there tinkering with his old cars as usual, radio blaring. Holly snuck past the doorway, anxious to avoid him at all costs. She reached the old barn, pulled open the creaking door and snapped on the light.

Immediately Emily's warm smell surrounded her. The cow's big face came up from her enclosure, and she stared at Holly with huge, soft eyes. Holly scratched Emily's forehead with one hand and rubbed viciously at her own tears with the other. Couldn't Mum see that it wasn't just Stonehenge that had made her crazy? Everything was shaking loose.

The barn was quiet, lit by a single bare bulb on the ceiling. It smelled of straw, cow dung, and old wood, and was cluttered with farm tools and shelves lined with paint cans and other junk. Aunt Sally said the barn was really old, built way back in the Middle Ages, and had been in the family for generations. It sure looked different from the barns Holly had seen back home; the walls were made of stone with high wooden beams inside that soared up like the inside of a church. The barn's roof was not made of shingles but of straw, or thatch, as Aunt Sally called it. She'd explained that the barn was built into the side of a hill in the old days before people had refrigerators. She had shown them a dark, earthy-smelling room cut into the hill itself, where boxes of vegetables, jars of canned fruit, and bottles of wine were stored.

Holly looked up into the darkness of the rafters. It was the height of the roof here that had made her think it might be a good place for music; she'd imagined the sound of her notes rising and echoing back to her, like in a cathedral. She put her recorder to her lips and played a couple of scales. *Hmm,* she thought. *Disappointing. Maybe further back . . .*

Holly moved inside, away from the Emily's stall and towards the storage room. She noticed that there was also a passage off to the left of this room, leading deeper into the hillside. She stepped forward for a closer look. Two rusting bicycles and a jumble of dusty boards half-filled the corridor, but she thought she glimpsed a door at the end of it. Mum had said to stay out front. But . . . it wouldn't hurt to just take a peek.

The tangle of junk she'd seen was actually a half-hearted barrier. Someone had painted the words *Keep Out* on a broken piece of wood and placed it facing the main room of the barn; but it had fallen down sideways beside a rusting baby carriage. Holly peered over the heap in front of her but couldn't see anything dangerous on the other side. There were lots of cobwebs along the walls; but nothing seemed about to collapse on top of her. *Why was Mum so in a knot about this place?* she wondered.

The light from the bulb above Emily's stall didn't reach very far down the corridor. Holly turned back to the shelves of junk and grabbed a dusty flashlight she'd noticed there; amazingly enough, it produced a feeble beam of light.

Holly shoved aside the pile of boards and stepped into the corridor beyond. That really *was* a door she'd seen. She walked a few steps, realizing as she did so that the corridor was dipping downward, leading her into the heart of the hill. The air was suddenly cold and damp. Here the walls were of white chalk, the chalk that made up the ground in this place. As she drew near the door, she heard a faint humming sound. She stopped to listen, then decided it must be Frederick's radio in the distance. Holly reached the old door and pulled on the corroded metal ring that served as a handle. The door wouldn't budge. Its hinges were badly rusted, and its wooden planks seemed held together by crumbling iron knobs. She ran her finger over one of these, and the pocked iron crumbled into red dust on her skin. Yet when she put down the flashlight and pulled on the ring with both hands, the door didn't even creak.

The humming sound was louder here. It was a high, sweet sound, almost like a human voice with no words. It reminded her of a recording she'd heard once of a wind harp set on a rocky beach, the haunting and ethereal sound of the breeze flowing through the harp strings untouched by a musician's hands. But where was this sound coming from? Holly shivered. She knew it couldn't be Frederick's radio. This was something else, something that made her skin prickle. Yet even as she stepped back uneasily, Holly found herself raising her recorder to her lips and improvising runs to the key of the hum. She couldn't stop herself.

Dad's face floated towards her. She could see him leaning on his cello, grinning at her.

"Piper," he said, *"some day you'll get so good that you'll lead the whole world off and away into some beautiful country we've never dreamed of."*

Click! Holly stopped playing. The old door stood ajar. The humming was much louder.

She stepped forward and gently pushed the door open a crack. Blackness lay beyond the threshold. A cold trickle of dread skittered down her spine. This was definitely weird. She stepped back a few paces and reached for the flashlight she'd set on the floor. Her heartbeat quickened. *I should get out of here!*

But the door stood open, the line of darkness beyond it

17

beckoning her like a long, thin finger. The melodic humming sound tumbled out and wrapped itself around her. She stood paralyzed for a moment, paralyzed and entranced. Then she forced herself to take a deep breath.

"It's just an old door, stupid," she told herself out loud. The sound of her voice made everything seem a bit better. But where was this music coming from? She nudged the door wide with her toe. The trembling beam of her flashlight spilled across the threshold and into a small, windowless room. Heart pounding, Holly drew a deep breath and stepped inside.

Like the storage room, it smelled of earth and moss and dampness. But unlike the other room, this one had a floor paved with fitted stones. It was empty except for a shelf on one wall with a row of covered clay pots on it. With a start Holly realized that it was these pots that were humming.

She stepped closer and ran a cautious finger along the side of one of them. The surface was rough and cool. Tucking her recorder into the back pocket of her jeans, she picked up the pot and carried it towards the door for a better look. She could feel the thrumming of the music inside it. The sound travelled through her bones and joints and made her whole body tingle. How could something made of clay be so alive?

"Holly? Are you here?" It was Mum's voice coming from the front of the barn.

Guilt seized her as she remembered her promise. Holly stepped backwards and turned an ankle on an uneven stone in the floor. She lost her balance and toppled over.

"No!" she cried out as the jar sailed out of her hands and back into the black shadows.

The pot shattered into a million shards on the floor. Like a flash of lightning, daylight filled the room. There was a boom of thunder and a mighty rush of wind. Holly screamed and closed her eyes against the storm that threatened to sweep her away.

When she opened them again, she lay face down on wet grass. Someone was singing. A shadowy figure moved towards her out of the mist.

CHAPTER THREE
BOREKAREK

"BARANU GRAKAT, BARANU TAKANI MAREGI . . ."

Holly stared at the moving shadow in panic as the chanting grew louder, closer. She scrambled to her feet. *Where am I? What happened?*

The wet grass had soaked the knees of her jeans and the front of her T-shirt. She tugged her jacket tighter across her chest and stood shivering, teeth chattering, ready to bolt.

The dark figure solidified as the mist shredded before it. It had a pair of pointed ears on its head and a long, flowing cloak below, ragged at the edges. It stopped and stared at her.

Holly screamed.

The figure had a wolf's head and a human body. The wolf's huge mouth gaped, displaying a row of gleaming teeth.

Holly spun around and ran. But the fog was thick, and she'd only covered a few yards when she stumbled and fell heavily to the ground. She struggled to her feet as the tall grey shape advanced out of the fog.

It stopped chanting and made other sounds. It halted just in front of her, mouth gaping wide.

"Do not be afraid." This time the sounds sorted themselves into words that Holly could understand, although she had the eerie feeling that they weren't English words.

Holly blinked, then blinked again. The wolf mouth was frozen open; it hadn't moved. And underneath its head was another face—a man's face. No, not a man. A boy. A boy with a bit of scruffy stubble on his face and a bad case of acne.

"Where did you come from?" he asked in a croaky voice.

"What do you mean where did *I* come from!" gasped Holly. "Where did *you* come from? Who are you?"

"The spell . . . ?" mumbled the boy. "But . . . you're just a boy!"

"I *am not!* I'm a girl! And what do you mean, 'spell'?" Holly felt the panic rising again.

"But . . ." he pointed to her head.

"What about my head? What does that have to do with anything?"

"You have your hair cropped like a warrior."

"A warrior?" Her heart was still pounding. "I'm not a warrior!" Then Holly had a sudden, happy inspiration. "It's you, Frederick, isn't it! I should have known! Give me that mask!" She lunged for it but the boy ducked away.

"Boy or girl, I have done wrong!" he said. "Borekarek will be furious! His anger will be that of the she-bear who has lost her cub!" He suddenly clapped his hands to his ears, closed his eyes and started moaning and swaying from side to side.

Holly stared at him. No, this wasn't Frederick. Frederick was weird, but not *this* weird. And the tufts of hair poking out from under the wolf mask were dark brown, not red. And where was the barn, the garage? She turned around, but saw nothing but fog. The boy howled more loudly.

"Please stop that," she said, plucking up her courage and tugging on the edge of his cloak. As she touched it, she realized it was the wolf's skin. The boy fell silent and looked at her warily.

"Please tell me what's going on. Why are you dressed up like this? And who is Buckaroo?"

"Borekarek is the great Sorcerer, the Seer and the Caller. I am his apprentice, and . . . I was practising a new spell," he said miserably.

She stared at him. "No, come on, really. Who are you, *really?*"

The boy looked baffled and a little hurt. "I have told you. You think I have spoken an untruth. A sorcerer's apprentice does not speak untruths."

Holly rubbed her clammy hands on her thighs. Surely this was a dream and she'd wake up any moment now. "Well then, where am I? Where is here?"

"You are standing at the foot of the Hill of the Sun Circle."

Holly shook her head. "I still don't understand," she said. "One minute I'm in the barn, the next I'm out here with you. What happened?"

The boy hung his head and stared at his feet. "I was saying a new spell. I had it all right, I know I did."

But spells are only in fairy tales. They don't exist in real life! Dad had explained this over and over when she was a little kid and eventually she had believed him, even though she didn't want to, and even though she always had the feeling he didn't quite believe it either.

She took a deep breath. "What spell?"

The boy studied his feet and said nothing.

"Aren't you allowed to say new spells?"

"It is a spell that is still forbidden to me. I looked at one of the secret rune-sticks." He looked up at her with a resentful pleading in his eyes. "But I had to! The invaders are coming and everyone knows what is foretold—that in the time of trouble we must do a Calling for the Maregi, the hero who will come and save us. Borekarek does not see how near the danger is, and so I did the Calling myself! But I must have done it wrong. . . ." He hung his head miserably.

Rune-sticks, invaders, a spell gone wrong. Had she stumbled into a video game? No, this was all too real for that. Holly's stomach clenched. The fog was thinning a little now, but there was no sign of the barn or the garage or Aunt Sally's house. Maybe she'd ended up down the road. . . .

"Look, just point me the way to Amesbury and I'll walk back myself."

He looked at her blankly. "I do not know this place."

Again Holly looked desperately around her. She could now see one edge of the horizon, but there was no sign of a town or any buildings in the distance. No sounds of traffic, no rumble of airplanes overhead. Only silence.

She grabbed the edge of the wolf-skin cloak and pulled on it. "Send me back!" she hissed through clenched teeth. "Whatever you just did, undo it! Send me back!"

The boy's face brightened. "Yes, of course! Borekarek does not know what I have done! He need never know!"

He fumbled in a skin pouch that hung at his side and pulled out a slender grey stick about six inches long. Holly could see long spidery lines carved into its smooth surface. The boy turned it over in his hands, tracing with one finger a mysterious pattern she couldn't see. After a moment he grew agitated and turned the stick over again, and again, over and over. He looked up at her in dismay.

"I cannot!" he croaked.

"You cannot *what?*"

"I cannot send you back! There is no spell here for sending the Maregi back!"

She stared at him. The panic almost choked her.

"But you have to!" she cried, gripping his shoulders and shaking him. "I have to get home! I don't belong here! Mum will think I've been kidnapped or something! And Dad . . . !" *I'll never see him again!*

She felt a hand on her shoulder. "Please," said the boy.

She gulped and rubbed at her eyes.

"I must take you to Borekarek. He may kill me for what I have done, but I must accept my punishment. Only he will know what to do."

Holly sniffed and raised her eyes to his. He looked as terrified as she was, but he had squared his scrawny shoulders and was trying to be brave.

"Follow me," he said. "It is not far."

Holly planted her heels in the soggy ground. "Where are we going? Shouldn't we stay here? What if I get lost?"

"I will lead you. We must see Borekarek. Come."

Holly hung back. *Maybe this kid really is crazy,* she thought. *Spells! For a minute there I actually believed him! If I could just get a clear view of the landscape, surely I could find my way back to the road that leads into town. . . .*

"You must come," the boy said solemnly.

She stopped squinting at the fog and took a long hard look at him. He wasn't like anybody she'd ever seen before, and his costume didn't look . . . like a costume. Instead of normal shoes, he wore some kind of leather wrappings on his legs and feet. And that wolf head—that looked very real.

Holly shuddered and fought back the fear. "Okay. Lead on."

She followed him up a long gentle slope. A wind had risen now and the mist was thinning fast. To the right she glimpsed dense copses of trees. They passed a place where the grass dim-

24

pled and a swift, narrow stream chattered through. Then the slope leveled off. The trees fell behind them, and they stepped onto a plateau. The fog blew past in tattered ropes. Holly suddenly stopped short, panting.

In front of her rose a cluster of massive stones. Her heart skipped a beat. It had to be Stonehenge.

The great pillars loomed out of the shredding mist. The crosspieces that joined them together at the top were all there, uniting the stones in a perfect circle like the rim of a wheel. The Heel Stone was upright, not slumped over as it was in all the pictures and drawings Holly had seen. The fence was gone, and there were no tourists.

She walked towards the stones as if pulled by an invisible thread. She passed between a pair of pillars and entered the circle, running her hand down the cool edge of the upright as she had longed to do this afternoon. She stood in the centre of the circle and turned slowly clockwise. Her skin tingled as if the air here were alive with electricity. The stones surrounded her on all sides, huge and silent, enclosing her in a fierce embrace.

She recalled her fantasy. Holly, High Priestess of the Sun God, decked out in her crimson robes. It seemed funny now, too pale compared to the wonder of these stones.

"Come!" the boy was shouting. "You must not stand there! It is a place of great power! Come!"

Slowly Holly turned towards him. But the circle seemed to hold her fast. Her legs felt heavy and slow. *He's right,* she thought, *there is power here.* It thrilled her and terrified her at the same time.

Then suddenly she was outside the circle and beside the boy again. He frowned at her and seemed about to say something, but turned and walked on.

She followed him to a low, round hut well beyond the circle, opposite the Heel Stone. Its walls were made of twigs and branches woven together, and its cone-shaped roof, which appeared much too large for it, was made of dried thatch. A thin finger of smoke pointed skyward from the hole in the centre of the roof.

The boy rapped three times on the doorpost. There was no door, but a heavy animal skin hung across the low opening. Holly heard a growl from within. The boy flung aside the skin and ducked inside. Holly followed, careful not to hit her head.

The hut had no windows, and it took a couple of minutes to get used to the gloom. A fire glowed in the middle of the room, and a huge metal pot was suspended above it. In the shadows beyond the fire Holly glimpsed a shaggy figure bent over something on a low table.

"Borekarek," croaked the boy, his voice cracking. "Forgive me, for I have made a terrible mistake. I did a Calling."

"Hmmph?" said the bulky shadow. Holly felt a stab of fear as she struggled to make sense of the shape in the gloom. It looked like an enormous bear. In fact, she saw, it *was* partly a bear. Like the boy, Borekarek wore an animal head on top of his own and used the skin as a cloak. The great bear's teeth gleamed fiercely in the firelight, and its empty eye sockets were black holes staring out at her.

"What Calling? For birds? Do not tell me you have summoned another army of deer!" growled the figure in a deep voice, straightening slowly until Holly marveled that he didn't hit the low ceiling beams.

"No, no. I . . . I called the Maregi."

"You *what?*" the old man roared. He lurched across the room with furious speed, raising a pair of claw-nailed hands in the air. He stopped in front of the boy and stood towering over him.

Holly screamed and shrank back, inching towards the doorway, ready to bolt. The wizard was a terrifying figure. His own grey hair stuck out from under the bear head in wild, matted clumps, and his eyes glittered with rage.

"You used the rune-sticks? Even when I forbade you? You would not have patience! You have disobeyed!"

"I know, I know!" yelped the boy, plastered against the wall beside Holly. "Please do not slay me! I will do anything for you to atone for my disobedience! Besides . . . someone came!"

"Someone *came?* Who? Maregi?"

"No . . . she did."

The wizard stopped, wheezing hard, and seemed to notice Holly for the first time. She shrank back even farther. But his anger seemed to evaporate when he saw her.

"She?" he growled. "This is a boy."

"She says she is a girl."

"Ah. Yes, yes, yes. . . ." He scratched his matted beard. "I have seen this age in the smoke of dreams. Yes." His greyish mouth curled back in a grin. Holly saw a set of very dirty, pointed teeth and caught a whiff of the rankest breath she had ever smelled. Yet he didn't seem quite so fearsome anymore.

"Tell me, young one, how did you get here?"

Holly drew a shaky breath and tried to remember. "I, uh . . . broke a pot. I found these pots and picked one up, but I dropped it—I didn't mean to, it just slipped—and when it smashed there was suddenly a storm in the room and then . . . then I was here . . . wherever here is. Please, you've got to get me back! Or just tell me which way Amesbury is and I'll walk. See, my aunt's house is there and I've got to get back."

"A pot?" muttered the wizard, eyes widening. "Korak's pots! I had forgotten them! Of course, there would not be a

Coming without a Sending. A Calling needs a Sending as well to work properly."

"The runes said nothing about pots," mumbled the boy under his breath.

The sorcerer fixed him with a smoldering glare. "You think I forbid you to try things you know nothing about for no reason? You have much to learn, young Evaken. Each working demands a knowledge of all the others. I must think of the right punishment for this misdeed of yours."

The boy shrank back again, wide-eyed, but the wizard made no move towards him. He was scratching his beard and muttering words that Holly could not understand.

Holly drew another ragged breath. "Please, sir," she said, "Please let me go back home. Or send me if you have to. I don't care about your Magee or whatever it is—I just have to go back."

"Yes, well, well," growled Borekarek, "I must think and remember. It has been a long time. . . . There must be a way, of course. Off with you both." He waved a bony hand. "Take our visitor home, Evaken, and have Avartha give her a good meal. I want both of you back here at sunset. By then I hope to understand what has happened."

"Come!" Evaken grabbed Holly's arm and yanked her through the doorway. They stumbled out into the light. Holly blinked back the tears as the brightness stung her eyes.

"Let go of me!" she shouted as he pulled her along.

He let go. She stopped and rubbed her wrist, then her eyes. The mist had burned off completely now, and she could scan the countryside on all sides. Everywhere she looked there were meadows and pockets of trees but no roads or houses. No people. No parking lot, no concession stand. No church spires rising in the distance. No Amesbury. Her stomach clenched. It was true then. She couldn't just walk back to the house because the house wasn't there.

Evaken walked on a few paces, then halted and looked back at her.

"Come," he growled.

"Where are we going?"

"To my home. Borekarek told me to give you food."

"I'm not hungry." Holly crossed her arms and eyed the trees at the bottom of the hillside. "I'm staying here until he sends me back home."

Evaken shrugged. "I cannot leave you here. I must obey Borekarek's commands."

Holly bit her lip. "Is it far?" she asked at last.

"No, not far."

"I'll only go with you if you *promise* to bring me back here as soon as we've eaten."

The boy shrugged again. "Very well." Without another word he turned and started down the slope ahead of her.

They walked steadily for at least an hour, most of the time following a little river that twisted across the plain. The sunlight lit the waving grass with gold. The sun warmed her up and dried her damp clothing, but her feet began to blister. What did Evaken mean, *not far?* And that knot of fear seemed to have settled into her stomach for good.

At last they reached a place where the rolling hills were dotted with clusters of round huts very much like Borekarek's. Smoke rose from the holes in their pointed roofs. Beyond them, a steeper hill with terraced steps rose up from the plain.

"What's that?" she pointed.

"Sarum."

"Sarum? What is it?"

"Our hill fort. Our refuge if we're attacked."

"Do you live there?"

"No!" he snorted. "We live here, on our farms. Come, this way."

He led her along a chalky path that forked off from the one that ran along the river. Soon she saw a group of buildings ahead. The low-growing shrubs by the path soon gave way to a clearing. Two large, round structures faced her and she saw that they were joined together. Three smaller huts stood off to one side.

A woman in a loose, knee-length dress was chopping wood outside one of the huts. Her long black hair, streaked with grey, hung in a disheveled rope down her back. She paused briefly to wipe the sweat from her brow and to return Evaken's nod of greeting, then caught sight of Holly and stared. Holly felt her face grow hot under the woman's suspicious gaze, and she was suddenly acutely aware of her jeans and bright blue T-shirt. The woman opened her mouth as if to call to Evaken, then abruptly closed it and turned back to her work. Her face was taut and lined with worry.

"Since our father died two winters ago, Mama and Avartha have been doing most of the work," he said. "Borekarek gives me leave to come some days."

"Your father . . . ?" Holly sucked in her breath.

"Yes," Evaken said shortly. "Come inside. Avartha will be here."

Like the wizard's house, this one also had a skin hanging in the doorway. Evaken pushed it aside and strode into the dimness. Holly followed more carefully, longing for that dim flashlight she had dropped in the barn. She hated not being able to see where she was going.

"Avartha!" called Evaken.

"Yes?" The voice was low, rich, musical. It belonged to a woman or perhaps a girl.

"I have news." Evaken moved off into the dimness.

Holly heard him whispering. She stayed near the doorway and the patch of light it allowed into the room. She blinked furiously, maddened at not being able to see. But she could smell, and her nose told her a good deal. The air was heavy with wood smoke and the aroma of boiling meat. There was the scent of unwashed bodies and wet wool drying and the deep, good smell of tanned leather.

Suddenly Holly realized she could see the fire in the centre of the room with a huge pot hanging over it. A *cauldron*, Dad would call it. Beyond the fire sat two figures. One was Evaken without his wolf-head and skin. The other was a girl about her age or maybe a bit older—a girl with hair as black as the shadows and eyes to match.

"Come!" the girl said, extending a hand to Holly in invitation.

Holly moved carefully across the room. It seemed cluttered; small humped shadows threatened every footstep. She reached the fire and sat down on a pile of skins beside the girl. Evaken stood and hovered awkwardly nearby.

"What is your name?" asked the girl, fixing her with amazing black, pool-like eyes.

"Holly."

"Ollee?" The name sounded strange on the girl's tongue.

"No, Holly. You have to breathe the *h* first. Holly."

"Hhh–ollee. I understand. A strange name."

"I'm—I guess I'm not from around here . . . unless you know a place called Amesbury." She sighed. It was worth one last try.

The girl shook her head. "My brother has told me what happened. You have come from far away. He called for the Maregi."

"Please tell me," said Holly, leaning forward. "Who is the Maregi? I don't understand anything."

"Maregi is the name of the one who will deliver us from our enemies. He is named in an old poem. Very ancient. It was given to the great seer Korak in a dream long ago. He remembered it and taught it to his people. Every child learns it at a young age."

"But who are your enemies? It seems pretty peaceful here."

Avartha sighed and gazed into the fire. The golden light played along a pair of strong cheekbones and a hard little chin. "We have not had any until now. The rhyme had become almost a game, a thing children chant at play. But now it is real. The wild men are coming from across the sea."

"Wild men? Who are they?"

"They are terrible. They have fine, hard weapons and strange fighting machines. They have long hair like women but are as fierce as wolves! They will destroy us!" Avartha shuddered and pulled nervously at the frayed corner of the woven shawl that she wore. "We need our deliverer now! We need our Maregi. And now, you are here at last." She looked up with a radiant smile.

Holly stared at her a moment as the words sank in. "No way! You've all made a mistake. I don't know how to save anybody!"

"It *is* confusing," said Avartha, chewing her lip. "We always thought the Maregi would be a man, but you are female. Yet you must be the Maregi. You come from a different place, yet you understand our language."

"I am *not* the Maregi!" Holly stood up shouting. "I'm not staying here! I just want to go home! Please, let me go home!"

"Come, Hhollee. . . ." Avartha clasped both hands around Holly's shaking wrists and pulled her back down onto the skins. "Maybe we are wrong, Hhollee. Perhaps you are not the one. Please, do not be so angry!"

Holly was sobbing now. "How will I get back home?" Even if Aunt Sally's house wasn't really home, it was better than this!

"I do not know," said Avartha, giving her hand a squeeze. "But I think that it will be revealed to you. Wait and see. Here," she ladled out some stew into a wooden bowl. "Eat now. You will feel better."

Avartha handed her the bowl and a flattened stick. Holly sniffed and rubbed at her tears. She poked the stick into the stew and managed to lift a bite to her mouth. The food was flavoured with unfamiliar herbs, but it didn't taste too bad.

"Hhollee, I must give you something," said Avartha, rising and moving away. Holly looked around for Evaken, but he had vanished. She thought she heard his voice outside. The rhythmic *chop, chop* of the mother's axe had stopped.

Holly set her bowl down on the floor and took the small object that Avartha placed in her hand. It was smooth and cool, like a stone.

"Here," said Avartha.

Holly held it closer to the firelight to see. "What is it?"

"It is an amulet. You must wear it always now. I carved it myself after I saw the bird in a dream."

"Bird?" Holly let the light play along the lines of the simple design. It was a squat bird with a sharp beak, in profile.

"It is a raven, a bird our people honour. The raven is the servant of the gods. Her image will protect you."

"Well, thank you, but—"

"Wear it!" Avartha's hands were suddenly at Holly's neck, tying the thin leather cord that held the amulet. She flicked the stone under the neckline of Holly's T-shirt.

33

"Okay, okay! I will!" Holly said in annoyance. "But I can't see what good it'll do. I don't know anything about your gods. . . ."

"You must wear it. The dream I had was frightening, very clear. . . ."

Suddenly Holly felt lightheaded. Avartha's words blurred together, like voices on a radio turned down low. She felt she hadn't quite grasped them. Her ears were buzzing.

"What did you say?" she asked. Her tongue felt like slush.

"Hhollee! Hhollee!" Avartha was shouting now. "Come back!" Her hand reached out to her. Holly tried to grasp it but she felt like she was drowning in a whirlpool. Her body seemed to dissolve around her mind. *I'm fainting,* she thought, *just like cousin Carla at Lisa's wedding. . . .*

The next moment she was lying face down on the stone floor of Aunt Sally's barn, blinking, breathless, her right hand curled around one jagged piece of the shattered pot.

CHAPTER FOUR
THE AMULET

"HOLLY? WHERE ARE YOU?" CAME MUM'S faint voice.

Holly struggled to her feet, heart pounding. Her arms and legs didn't seem to be working right. She gripped the wall as dizziness threatened to engulf her. But she had to move! Mum was out there, and she was *in here*—here where she wasn't supposed to be. She grabbed the flashlight and lurched out of the room, pulling the heavy old door shut behind her.

"Here!" she called as loudly as she could. Her voice sounded high and tight. She walked towards the light of the bare bulb, dimly aware of the lingering taste of lamb stew and an unfamiliar weight around her neck.

"Holly?"

"I said, I'm here!" Holly stepped out into the main room of the barn. Mum stood staring at her for a moment, then suddenly strode forward, eyes flashing. She grabbed Holly by the shoulders and shook her.

"Holly! What did I tell you about going in there! How dare you disobey me when you promised not to!"

Holly shrank back. "I—I'm sorry, I know I

35

said I'd stay out here, but I just went to take a peek, honest! I was only in there a minute." *It was only a minute, wasn't it? So then what was all that stuff that happened?*

"Then what's all this dirt on your jeans, on your shirt?" Mum flicked an angry finger at the T-shirt.

Holly looked down as the memories flooded back. The wet muddy grass, the fog.

"I—I did trip, and I sort of fell on the floor, but I didn't get hurt, really! I'm fine—"

"Holly, listen to me," said Mum, cupping Holly's face in her hands and bringing her face close to hers, "I mean what I say. It is *very dangerous* in there. I know, because I had some close calls when I was a kid. That's why the passage was blocked off. Don't you ever, *ever* go in there again, do you hear me?"

Holly gazed into Mum's crackling blue eyes in shock. Mum never got this angry—*never.* Was there something else here, something that went way beyond fear for Holly's safety? As if she almost knew. No. Impossible.

Holly drew a deep breath. "I promise. I'll never go in there again if you're so freaked about it. I *promise!"*

Mum let go of her and turned away. Her shoulders rose and fell in quick breaths. "I don't want to hear of any more practice sessions in here, do you hear me?"

"Okay. For sure. No problem." Holly's heart was pounding so hard she was sure Mum could hear it.

"Let's go inside. Sally's made some tea, and there's a show on TV that you might be interested in."

"Okay." Holly walked towards the door. She suddenly felt an arm around her shoulder, gentle now. She almost flinched, but it felt good too.

"Listen, Holly, I'm . . . I'm sorry I jumped on you like that.

It just got me . . . remembering, that's all. I just don't want you to get hurt."

"Forget it, it's okay."

They walked in silence back to the house. Holly's mind was spinning. *What happened in there? Did I knock myself out when I fell?*

They walked swiftly through the wet grass, past the garage where the radio still blared. Holly could hear the voices of Frederick and his dad over the clink and clang of tools. The noise made her want to cry for joy; it was so *normal*. She remembered the eerie silence of that other place. . . . Her knees were shaking.

"Better get that dirty shirt off," said Mum as she swung the back door open.

Without a word, Holly strode down the hall to the bedroom. Inside, she pulled off the shirt and rummaged in her suitcase for a new one. The jeans weren't too bad; the knees had dried out now and much of the dirt just rubbed off. She caught sight of herself in the mirror as she lifted her arms to pull a clean shirt over her head. She froze. The amulet.

It glowed black against her pale skin. Holly felt its weight, its coolness. She began to tremble.

I really was there. It wasn't a dream.

She stood staring at her reflection, paralyzed.

"Holly?" came Mum's voice from the living room. "The show's starting."

Automatically, Holly pulled the clean shirt over her head, flicked the amulet inside the collar, and headed out the door.

Aunt Sally was curled up in the big easy chair in the living room with the TV on. A cup of tea steamed beside her. She turned and grinned.

"Cup o' tea for you, Holly?" In one swift movement she

was out of the chair, into the kitchen and pouring tea into a flowered mug.

"Yes, please."

"There's biscuits as well. Here we are. Help yourself." She thrust a round package of chocolate-covered cookies into Holly's hands.

Mum was settled in on the couch. "Look, Holly," she said, "It's all about the people who built Sarum in medieval times."

The images on the TV caught her attention. There was an artist's reconstruction of the castle as seen from the air, then a modern-day picture of the ruined walls.

"Wow!" she said.

"Holly's turning out to be a real history buff like her dad," Mum said lightly to Aunt Sally.

"We shall have to go out to Old Sarum before your mum leaves, Holly," said Aunt Sally. "It's only a hop, skip, and a jump from here, you know."

Although she tried, Holly couldn't focus on the TV program. Her hands were shaking so much that she almost spilled her tea. She had a feeling this stuff about Sarum might be important, but she couldn't concentrate. Images drifted back to her, smacking her like snowflakes. The fog, the reeking gloom of Borekarek's hut, Avartha's eyes, the Stones. And then Mum's fury, so sudden and so strange.

She forced herself to watch the TV. They were talking about the medieval castle now. It was crowded with people and horses and carts, and it didn't look much like the hill-fort she had seen with Evaken.

Evaken!

Did I really meet him? Or did I dream it all?

The chocolate coating on her cookie melted between her fingertips, and it slid down onto her right knee. She brushed at the chocolate stain, then noticed how well it blended in with the dried mud. Maybe Aunt Sally wouldn't notice it. She was glad the volume was turned up, that both Mum and Aunt Sally seemed to be so into this show, so she didn't have to talk to them. But she couldn't keep her mind on anything.

Suddenly the credits were rolling and the program was over.

"Cor!" exclaimed Aunt Sally as she leaned over to push the off button. "Fancy living back then! No running water, no electricity. Hard to imagine, isn't it?"

"It sure is," agreed Mum, setting down her empty teacup. "But they seem to have been able to do a lot of things in spite of what they didn't have."

"You'd have to be resourceful, wouldn't you?" Aunt Sally got up and bustled out to the kitchen with the cups.

"Mum, I'm really, really tired," said Holly, getting up from the couch. "I'm going to bed."

"You do that, honey," said Mum with a strained smile. "We could go out to Old Sarum tomorrow morning and see it up close, if you like. My plane doesn't leave until six."

Holly gulped. "Sure, if you like. Whatever. Well, good night." She slipped through the door and poked her head into the kitchen. "Good night, Aunt Sally. And thanks for the tea and those great cookies."

"Ah, you're most welcome, love. Ni' night."

Holly hurried down the hall to the bedroom and leaned the door shut. She sank down onto the floor and buried her head in her arms. The whole world was spinning.

She tried to remember everything that had happened there, wherever *there* was. *Something about calling and sending, magic runes, a poem about a hero. And Stonehenge, a different Stonehenge.* Was it a dream? No. Her hand found the amulet around her neck and glided over its polished edges. No, not a dream. If not, then what?

Suddenly she remembered Dad's book. She lurched to her feet and snapped on the light. It was lying on her bed, where she'd dropped it when Mum came in.

Holly sat on the bed and flipped through the chapters on Stonehenge. There were lots of photographs and diagrams of the stone circle at various stages. But it was only in the diagrams that the circle was complete, with all the crosspieces fitted together around the top. In all the photos there were pieces missing. So what did that mean?

The ebb and flow of conversation in the living room distracted her. Mum and Aunt Sally were talking earnestly, *again,* in voices they thought were too low for her to hear.

"It's only for three weeks. Then she'll be home again. . . ." Mum's voice floated in through the cracks in the old wallpaper, into this room where she and Aunt Sally had slept when they were kids. Holly had no trouble imagining Aunt Sally as a kid, but Mum. . . . Even in the picture of the two of them on the mantel, Mum always looked old. Serious.

And why didn't Mum have an English accent? Had she left England so long ago that she'd lost it? Holly had never thought about it before at home, but here the difference between her and Aunt Sally really stood out. Come to think of it, that wasn't the only difference. . . .

"Right," came Aunt Sally's voice again, "and then you'll have a kid who's *really* angry. You can't run away from it this time, Gillian."

"I am *not* running away!"

"It nearly broke Dad's heart, when you left—"

"Sally! How could you?" Mum's voice dropped even further. "You don't know the real reason why—"

"I know more than you think. And this time it's different. If you're not careful, your plans to make it easy on her will be totally scuppered. . . ."

Make what easy on me? Holly gritted her teeth and willed herself to look at the book. Dad's voice came back to her.

"These are the bluestones," he said, pointing, "the first stones that people put on the site. Some think these stones marked the movements of the sun and moon, so the people could keep track of the seasons."

"Sort of like a calendar?"

"Something like that."

What had Evaken called it? The Hill of the Sun Circle.

"You really must tell her, Gillian. It's not fair." Aunt Sally's voice was low and intense.

"How can I tell her when I don't know for sure? *That* wouldn't be fair."

Tell me what? Holly wondered as her stomach knotted again. Then it came to her. *Oh, oh no, not that!*

Viciously she turned the pages of the book, blinking back tears, trying to conjure up Dad's face, his voice, his calm presence.

"See these?" he said. "These huge stones were put up by some other people, much later. Maybe they wanted it to be a temple as well as a calendar. Nobody knows for sure."

"Were they the Druids?"

"No!" Dad chuckled. "Don't listen to all that stuff about Druids. The Druids were Celts, but these people weren't. The stones were put there long before the Celts came to Britain. They may have used the site later on, but they certainly didn't build it."

The people who built Stonehenge weren't Celts. Then who were they?

Suddenly she snapped the book shut and tossed it into the

jumble of clothes in her suitcase. *Who cares who they were?* she thought furiously. *It won't make a bit of difference to my life, to Mum and Dad.*

She threw herself on the bed and allowed the tears to come. She let the terrible word seep through her whole body. *Divorce.* Were Mum and Dad getting a divorce? Was that what this crazy trip was all about? Was that what Aunt Sally wanted Mum to tell her?

Holly turned off the light and undressed. Her hands touched the amulet again. It was wondrously cool, despite having been next to her warm skin. What had Avartha said? That it would *protect her.* From what? From being left here with these relatives she barely knew? From the trouble between Mum and Dad? From being so alone?

Holly curled up in her little bed by the window and stared out at the dark sky. The clouds were breaking up, and a ragged moon struggled to shine. Sleep would not come. She was still awake long after Mum had crept into the bed opposite and the night had settled about the old house.

It was only as sleep finally tugged at her that Holly remembered her recorder. She had left it inside that room in the barn. The room with the pots.

CHAPTER FIVE
RAVENS

WHEN HOLLY FINALLY SLEPT, SHE DREAMED the dream again. The black and white mountains were all around her. She saw her hands groping in front of her as she picked her way up a rocky path through the tangle of evergreens.

Then she was suddenly through the pass. Before her rippled a land of rolling hills and waving grasses. It too was shadowed like the mountains, as if a bitter cloud were blocking the sun. . . . And then the shadow lifted for a brief moment, and Holly heard the rushing sound of wings above her, beating, beating, swooping down, roaring in her ears until there was nothing else. . . .

She sat up, screaming.

"What is it, honey?" The shadows coalesced into the dim shape of Mum's face. Her hand was cool on Holly's forehead.

"A—a dream, I guess . . ." Holly was panting hard.

"Just a dream. It's okay, sweetheart, you're here now, you're safe. Go back to sleep. It was just a dream. . . ." Mum stroked Holly's forehead as she repeated the words over and over.

"Just a dream," Holly mumbled. She sank

back into sleep as the thunder of wings faded into the distance.

HOLLY WOKE with the sun streaming across her bed. Sleep still weighed on her, and the memory of all those wakeful hours in the dark crept back. Holly groaned and rolled over. Mum's bed was empty and already made. On top of it sat a blue suitcase filled with neatly folded clothes. Holly pounded the bed with her fist. *Today. She's leaving today.*

Aunt Sally was flipping strips of bacon in the kitchen when Holly came out. Mum was carefully spreading marmalade to the edges of a piece of cold toast. Holly sat down and slipped a slice out of the toast rack. She would *never* get used to eating cold toast.

"Morning!" said Aunt Sally. "Eggs and bacon?"

"Um, I guess . . . yes, please," muttered Holly. How could anybody be that cheerful all the time? And especially *today*. . . .

"That must have been some dream you had last night," Mum said. "You got back to sleep okay?"

"Oh . . . yeah, pretty soon." Holly buttered her toast with great concentration, nudging the glistening yellow right to the edge, smoothing it out over and over.

"Good. You screamed, and I wondered—"

Suddenly it was all too much. "Mum—forget the dream. How long before I get to come back too?"

Mum sighed and looked away. "Three weeks. You know that, Holly. You've got your return ticket in your bag."

"Three weeks is *forever*, Mum. *Please*, can't I come back sooner than that?"

"You know that's impossible, honey. We've already paid for your ticket. And besides, our reservation at the resort is for three weeks."

"Right, like Godzilla or some space aliens are going to strike you dead if you leave a few days early!"

"Holly! Come on, you're acting like a child. . . ."

"Right! Here we are at last!" Aunt Sally set down a steaming plate of scrambled eggs and bacon in front of each of them.

Holly stared at the mess on her plate. The scrambled eggs were greasy mountain peaks, the bacon strips were glistening streams, and the thunder of wings came back to her. Then the smell of grease hit her, and Holly's appetite evaporated.

"I thought we'd leave for Old Sarum around ten," said Aunt Sally. "That'll give us time to walk round and look at everything and then have some lunch in town. Maybe walk round the shops as well. How's that?"

"Mmm," nodded Holly, only half listening. Maybe another slice of toast. . . .

"Sounds lovely, Sally," said Mum. "You've been awfully kind chauffeuring us around like this."

"Don't be daft! You've been away long enough to earn the royal tour!"

They left soon after breakfast. To Holly's annoyance, Frederick came with them too. He didn't look any happier about it than she was, but his mother had clearly given him no choice.

There was no mistaking the hill when it came into view. A moat encircled a steep bank that rose in terraces above the fields. They drove up a narrow road between low bushes and tufts of long grass, then through a cut in the chalky bank. Beyond it was a parking lot. As Aunt Sally pulled the car into one of the spaces, a startled flock of black birds rose shrieking into the air. Holly jumped and stifled a scream.

"Y'awright then, love?" said Aunt Sally, putting an arm around her as she got out of the car.

"Yeah, I'm fine. Just startled me, that's all." *Those dreams are making me jumpy,* she thought grimly.

"Well, here we are then," said Aunt Sally. "There's not much left of the Norman castle. None o' those handsome blacksmiths like on telly last night, I'm afraid!"

They walked in silence up the hill and across a wooden bridge that spanned a second deep ditch. Then they climbed the path that led inside the inner bank.

They had to pay to get in here too, but this place didn't feel at all like Stonehenge. For one thing, there was nobody else here on this sunny morning. No crowds, no noisy buses. Holly breathed deeply of the rain-washed air and strolled across the circular lawn towards a series of ruined walls.

"These are what's left of the medieval buildings," said Mum, pointing to a wall of crumbling stone and mortar.

"What about the really old buildings, the prehistoric ones?" asked Holly, "Are they still here somewhere?"

"Underneath all the layers of Roman and medieval stuff, I expect," said Aunt Sally. "You can't see them now. But those prehistoric fellows built this whole mound in the first place, with the two deep ditches we crossed."

"It's amazing they could have done all that with pickaxes made of deer's antlers and wooden shovels, like they said on the show last night," Mum said.

Holly veered away and ran up the steep slope to the overgrown edge of the fortress wall. The strong breeze caught her as she reached the top. She crouched, catching her breath. Below, the vast patchwork of green and golden fields swelled and dipped away on all sides. It was quiet here; there was only the low whisper of the wind in the long grasses, the cries of birds, the faint hum of cars on the road below. *But not as quiet as that other place,* Holly realized with a shiver.

This place seemed too empty. Disappointing, just like Stonehenge. *What did you expect?* she scolded herself. She hadn't even heard of Sarum until yesterday. But then, so much had happened yesterday.

She turned away, then stopped. Frederick stood on the slope just below her, scowling.

"What's the matter now?" he mumbled, squinting up at her.

"Nothing!"

"It's never good enough for you, is it? Not quiet enough, not old enough. You looking for Druids, then? The ones as built Stonehenge?"

"There weren't any Druids at Stonehenge, stupid. It's way older than that."

"Oh, pardon me. What is it you want, then?"

"You wouldn't understand what I want!" she growled.

"You'll just have to make the best of it, won't you? Like the rest of us."

"I shouldn't have to! I shouldn't even be here!"

"No use moaning about it. You'll drive us all crackers wanting to see things that aren't here."

"What do you know about it? Just shut up, will you!" She stormed past him and ran down the slope to the gate where Mum and Aunt Sally were buying postcards.

She took a deep breath and leaned against the kiosk wall, forcing down the fury inside her. How was she going to live with Frederick for three weeks? Dizzy from anger and lack of sleep, she stared at her feet as she followed the others back to the car.

Salisbury was a bustling town. They wound their way down the narrowest lane Holly had ever seen and suddenly emerged near a large square. Aunt Sally zipped into a tiny parking space.

"Want to have a look round the shops?" she asked.

"I'd like to take a last stab at finding a dress, Sally, if we have time," said Mum, climbing out.

"This is a lovely shop." Aunt Sally pointed to the one in front of them.

"Holly, do you want to come in?"

"Nah . . ." She gazed out the busy square.

"Stay close by then. We'll be in here."

"Sure." Holly wandered out into the square. Frederick had already disappeared into the crowd. It was market day, and the large open area was packed with rows of stalls. Holly slipped in among the hordes of shoppers buying everything from vegetables to cheap watches. On one corner a man boomed "Potatoes—ten pound for a pound!" Another stall was lined with long tubes filled with buttons of all colours.

Holly wandered over to a stall that sold something called cockles, then noticed Frederick at the booth next door. He stood, shoulders hunched, hands in his pockets, gazing pensively at an assortment of fish. They were whole, with scales glistening in the sun and milky eyes staring out into space.

"Used to eat fish all the time in Portugal," he mumbled.

Holly started. She hadn't expected him to speak to her again.

"What was it like in Portugal?" she asked uneasily, sidling a bit closer.

"Fantastic. Blue water, warm all the time. Don't know why we had to come back here. All it ever does is rain." He didn't look at her, just stared at the fish as if they might slap their tails and slip away if he took his eyes off them.

"True." She searched for something more to say, but couldn't think of anything. She was not going to apologize for being rude at Old Sarum. *He started it!* Obviously, he wasn't about to apologize either. Fine.

She drifted away, and he didn't seem to notice. In the next stall a woman with long black hair was selling curious old jewellery, and Holly poked through piles of strange and twisted shapes: crescent moons, stylized trees, snarling animals. At first she fingered the objects absent-mindedly, then slowly became aware that she was looking for something. *For what?* She glanced up to find the woman watching her closely. Their eyes met and the woman flashed her a smile that made Holly shiver. Quickly she turned back to the jewellery and unearthed a small silver brooch shaped like a bird taking flight. It was badly tarnished, and the jewel that had evidently formed its one eye had fallen out. Yet Holly couldn't put it down. There was something about it. . . .

"A raven, I think," said the woman. "Lovely trinket, in't it?"

A raven. Holly caught her breath.

"How much?" she heard herself say.

"Only a pound, love. Here, I'll wrap it up for ye."

Before she realized it, Holly was dropping a one-pound coin into the woman's palm and had slipped the tissue-wrapped brooch into her pocket.

"Holly!" She glanced up. Mum and Aunt Sally were beckoning her from across the road. Frederick slouched near them. Holly followed them down the street to a restaurant built inside an old mill. There was still a waterwheel, and a pond with ducks and swans floating on it.

"Isn't this lovely!" said Mum as they took their seats.

Holly stared at the birds on the water. *At least they're not ravens,* she thought.

Lunch was a blur. Mum and Sally laughed and joked about how much the town had changed since they were school girls. Holly sat silently picking at the salad on her plate, dimly aware that Frederick was doing the same. She shifted in her seat and felt a stab of pain in her right thigh. The brooch! She pulled it out of her pocket, unwrapped it and turned it over. Why had she spent a whole pound on this thing? It wasn't even that pretty. She gazed at the empty eye socket uneasily and realized with a start that it reminded her of the vacant eyes of the wolf and bear heads that Evaken and Borekarek had worn. But there was something else too. The wing—that was it. Wings beating . . . her dream . . . She shuddered.

"What's that, Holly?" Mum looked over.

"Just an old brooch I bought at the market." Holly closed her fingers over it, suddenly unwilling to show it to anyone.

"Let's see, honey." Mum tugged it out of Holly's hand and studied it. "Interesting shape."

"Poor bird's lost his eye," said Aunt Sally, leaning closer. "I have some sparkly bits at home in my sewing basket. We could glue a new eye in."

"Maybe." Holly held out her hand. "Please . . . can I have it back?"

Mum glanced at her quickly, then handed over the brooch. Holly quickly stuffed it back into her jeans, noticing at the same time that her thigh was stinging where the brooch's sharp pin had pricked her.

When they arrived home, Uncle Ian was cleaning out the trunk of his car.

"'Allo!" he greeted them with his big crinkly grin. "Nice lunch?"

"Really lovely," smiled Aunt Sally.

"I'll just go finish packing," said Mum, hurrying inside.

Holly was left standing by the side door. Frederick had already slunk around the corner to the garage in the back.

"Here, Holly," said Aunt Sally, "Your mum will want to pack her new things." She handed Holly two silver plastic bags from the dress shop.

"I hope you don't mind not going to the airport, Holly," said Mum when she walked into the bedroom. "You know how far away Heathrow is and how early I have to be there. You'd have nothing to do for all that time, and you wouldn't get home until late. It's better this way."

"Yeah, I know. It's *better* this way." Holly tossed the bags at Mum's suitcase and sank down on her bed.

"Holly," said Mum in a tight voice, walking towards her. Holly stared at the floor and willed the tears back as the arms closed around her.

"How can you do this to me?" Holly choked out. "I'd never take off and leave *my* kid! Never!"

"Holly, I don't *want* to leave you, but I have no choice. Dad and I need some time alone together, and there's no other family at home to take you in. It was either this or camp . . . and we both thought it would be good for you to get to know your own family here. You saw too little of Granny and Grand-dad while they were still alive."

"And whose fault was that? Mine?"

"Of course not! It was nobody's fault, really . . . or it was mine if it was anyone's. The point is, this is the best place for you right now. Sally is a great person, and you'll make friends with Frederick. . . ."

"No, I *won't*. He hates me!"

"Frederick has had a hard time readjusting to life in England. He hasn't made many friends. He probably feels a lot like you do."

"I don't care. He's a grump."

"Well, even if you don't make friends with him, Aunt Sally has some time off and she'll be able to take you places. You've always wanted to see England, haven't you?"

"Yeah, but not all by myself!"

51

"You won't be by yourself, honey! I'm really sorry it has to happen this way, but I don't see an alternative."

Holly glared at the watercolour painting on the far wall and concentrated on the way her unshed tears made it flicker.

"Come on, give me a kiss." Mum's arms enfolded her and Holly buried her face in the white linen shirt. "Be a good girl now. Three weeks isn't so long."

"Yeah, sure."

She gave Holly another squeeze, then thrust the silver bags into the suitcase. "That's about it. I think I've got everything." She picked up the suitcase and carried it out the door.

When Holly finally stepped outside, the suitcase was in the trunk of the car and Mum was busy hugging Aunt Sally. She stood miserably on the step. *This is it. She's really, really leaving.*

"Holly!" called Mum, arms wide.

Holly stepped into them. *Linen. Perfume. Don't go, don't go!* The beat of dark wings pounded in her head again.

"Say hi to Dad for me," she whispered.

"I will. See you soon, honey."

Then the lithe form in the trim yellow suit was in the front seat of the car. Mum's hand waved as the car backed out of the driveway. Everyone was waving. A flood of desolation washed over Holly as the car disappeared down the road.

"Cup o' tea, love?" smiled Aunt Sally, laying an arm on her shoulder.

"Uh . . . I don't know. . . ."

"I'll make a pot and you can join me if you like. Awright?" She disappeared inside.

Holly sank down on the crumbling front step of the house and stared at the empty road. She was alone. She buried her head in her hands, past tears now. And tired, so very tired.

What was that last thought that had jolted her awake last

night? The recorder. She'd left her recorder in the barn. *Stupid!* But then she'd been so confused, and Mum was calling her.

So why not just go back and get it? No big deal, right? *Right. But what if something happens again in there, like it did yesterday?* Holly shuddered.

But she couldn't imagine living for three weeks without her recorder. She loved its simple, hollow sound. Playing her recorder was always such a comfort. She'd never survive here without it.

She stood up and walked towards the barn.

The door was open and Emily was outside in the paddock, grazing. Light poured in through the doorway and through the cracks in the old roof high above her. Her foot struck something hard, and she saw it was the flashlight she'd dropped when Mum grabbed her. She bent and picked it up, switched it on.

I'll just be a second, Holly told herself as she nudged past the junk in the old passageway. *I'll just reach in and grab it, and run in and out.*

She reached the door with a sigh of relief. No music today. She stepped forward, but something on the floor caught her eye.

There in the corner by the rough-hewn chalk wall, half-buried in dust, lay a recorder.

But not her recorder.

Holly stooped and picked it up gingerly. It was ivory-coloured, but grey now with dust and cobwebs. How many years had it been here? She blew at it and layers of dust flew off. The mouthpiece was caked with dirt. She picked at it with her fingernail and the grime fell away. Holly rubbed it clean on her shirt. Who left it here? Without thinking, she raised it to her lips and blew. A long, clear note sounded. It seemed to echo through the whole barn.

That note was answered by another, and another. All in unison. All from within the room with the pots.

The door creaked, and swung open.

Holly screamed.

Chapter Six
Raiders

Holly lurched back and dropped the recorder, then whirled and stumbled back along the passageway. As she burst into the dim light of the barn, her foot caught the edge of the old baby carriage and she went sprawling on the dirt floor. *Whump!* Dust and straw and grit flew up and coated her face, her teeth. She lay coughing and gasping for breath as the music looped itself around her, tugging at her. She clapped her hands over her ears.

"*No!*" she yelled out loud. "*I'm not going back!*"

But she knew it wasn't true. She knew it. The music was too strong for her.

Holly scrambled to her feet, breathing hard. Her legs started walking, moving her back towards the inner room, towards the pots. *No, no, no!* she screamed to herself, but her legs kept moving.

The shards of the first pot lay on the floor. There were three pots left on the shelf. *Maybe nothing will happen this time,* she thought. She knew that wasn't true either.

Holly watched her hands reach out and pick up the second pot. She felt its vibrating coolness in her hot palms. The pot was so alive that it almost leaped out of her hands. It crashed to the floor and a fist of wind knocked her over.

She buried her head in her arms until the wind abated. Then she slowly looked up.

The sun beat down on a grassy field scented with the sweet smells of clover. Far off, to her left, she could hear the whisper of the river and some children laughing. Nearby a bird called.

She sat up and blinked in the brightness. This wasn't Stonehenge. Before her stood a cluster of houses that looked familiar. She glimpsed a movement beside one of the round buildings. A black-haired girl in dark clothing was seated on a block of wood, dropping a whirling spindle and guiding a snake of brownish fuzz onto it. Holly watched the spindle dip and rise in a whirring blur. Avartha.

She stood up slowly. *I could just stay here and watch,* she told herself. *Not get involved. Not let anyone know I'm here. I don't want to be here! If I can't fight the power that brings me here, at least I can refuse to do anything!*

But there was something in Avartha's movements that tugged at her. A sadness, a tense longing. For what?

Holly drew a deep breath. "Avartha!" she called.

Avartha dropped the spindle and stared. The sadness on her face changed to alarm, then joy. She leaped up and ran towards her, cloak billowing like a sail. She threw her arms around Holly, who returned the embrace and decided that she liked the mingled smells of wood smoke, cooking fat and sweet herbs in Avartha's hair.

"Hhollee! Hhollee!" It was almost a sob. "We have been waiting so anxiously!" Avartha drew back and fixed Holly with her dark eyes. It was then that Holly noticed a large bruise on Avartha's cheek. She gasped.

"Avartha, what happened to you?" She reached out a finger.

Avartha drew back quickly. "It is nothing. Why did you leave?"

"What do you mean it's nothing? It must hurt! What happened?"

Avartha sighed in exasperation. "I was careless yesterday in milking the goats and my mother punished me. Why did you leave so suddenly before Borekarek summoned you? You changed into mist before my eyes, and I could not hold you!"

Holly gaped at her in horror as she tried to visualize the blow coming down hard on Avartha's face. A horrible, ugly bruise! Mum had never done anything like this to her. Neither of her parents would.

"Hhollee! Why?" Avartha was shaking her impatiently.

"Um . . ." Holly forced herself to remember, recalling only the sensation of dissolving into the air. "I didn't mean to go. I just started to disappear and I couldn't do anything."

"You must see Borekarek at once." Avartha grabbed Holly's hand and pulled her along the dirt path that led from the yard to the river road.

"I was only gone one day! You're lucky I came back at all! I sure didn't want to!"

Avartha stopped and looked at her blankly. "Holly, it is a full moon-cycle since we saw you last."

Holly caught her breath. "You mean a whole month? That's—that's impossible!" *Unless time is different here.*

"Avartha," she said slowly, "I don't understand. I was here only yesterday. I don't understand how this works. All I did was break the pots."

"What pots?" Avartha glanced at her sideways as she pulled her forward again.

"There are some clay pots in a secret room I found. The first time I broke one accidentally, I came here. And it happened again just now."

"Hmm," Avartha frowned. "Evaken says Borekarek has been muttering about Korak's vessels."

"Korak? Isn't that the guy who talked about the Maregi?"

"Yes." Avartha frowned. "Borekarek has been studying the words of the prophecy and reading the magical runes day and night. We need help soon, for there is word of more raids on the homesteads that lie towards the sunrise."

Raids on the homesteads . . . Holly shivered. She wasn't sure what that meant, but it didn't sound good. She glanced over at Avartha's face; her lips were set in a straight, determined line.

"Listen," Holly said, swallowing hard, "I'm not this Maregi of yours."

Avartha fixed her with her dark eyes. "You must be. You returned. Only the Maregi would return."

"But I didn't want to! I was dragged here. I didn't have a choice!"

Avartha's mouth twitched in a grim smile. "Ah! The pull of fate! That is all the more reason to believe you are the Maregi."

Holly felt her cheeks redden. "No! I'm—"

"Wait, Hhollee. Wait and hear what Borekarek has to say."

By the time they reached Borekarek's hut the sun was high overhead and Holly was hot and tired.

Avartha rapped on the doorpost. In a moment Evaken's wolf head appeared from the inner gloom behind the door-skin. His human eyes blinked at them beneath the gaping jaws.

"Evaken," said Avartha. "Hhollee has returned. She is here with me."

Evaken let out a whoop and disappeared inside.

In a moment they heard a satisfied roar from within the hut. Evaken reappeared, gesturing wildly for them both to enter. Holly took a deep breath and ducked inside.

The sorcerer's hut was even darker than Holly remembered. A bitter-smelling brew of some kind bubbled over the glowing coals of the fire. The bear shape lumbered towards her out of the deep shadows.

"Welcome!" rumbled Borekarek, stopping a few feet away from her. He stood there for a moment, saying nothing. Holly guessed he was studying her, but since she could see little in the dimness she couldn't be sure.

"You have chosen your destiny and have returned."

"No way! I haven't *chosen* anything! I didn't want to come back here! I keep trying to tell you I'm not the one you think I am! I only went back to get my recorder because Mum just left me and—"

"No." The great bear head was moving slowly from side to side. "You have come because you were *meant* to come. You are the Maregi."

"I'm telling you it's all a big mistake!" She searched desperately for Evaken's face in the gloom.

"It was no mistake," said Borekarek, moving nearer. "Evaken and I have studied the rune-sticks, and it is clear that he did not chant the wrong spell. He did a Calling for the Maregi. And Maregi came."

Holly clenched her fists. "You don't understand! I'm no hero. I can't do anything to help you against any invaders. I can't fight, I don't know how to make swords or anything. . . ."

"There are many ways of fighting and of winning," growled Borekarek. "I will tell you what is prophesied about you, young Maregi. You do not know it yet, but you possess great power. Listen."

Borekarek moved closer to the glowing fire and stretched out his gnarled hands. Light played along the deep lines on his face as he closed his eyes. To Holly's amazement, he began to chant.

> *When night eats the moon*
> *and smoke fills the skies,*
> *when men sleep at noon*
> *with the sun in their eyes,*
> *when blood fills the cup*
> *and all laughter dies*
> *Call the Maregi: Maregi will come.*
> *Four winds will moan at Maregi's call.*
> *The moon and stars will be held in thrall.*
> *Sky-flames will dance to the beat of black wings,*
> *Midnight and dawn as Maregi sings.*
> *One voice calls them and one voice binds*
> *darkness to light as the shadow unwinds.*
> *One hope holds them, the two and the one.*
> *Black wings beat at the jaws of the sun.*
> *Call the Maregi: Maregi will come.*

A sharp tingle raced down Holly's spine. She felt her mind float out on the rhythmic waves of that voice, like a twig carried along on a mighty tide. The words were crazy, mysterious, wonderful. Somehow she knew that the language being spoken was not her own—and yet was open to her. Even after Borekarek had fallen silent, the words seemed to linger around him, suspended in a web of magic and firelight and breathless air.

Holly blinked and tried to focus her eyes on the old wizard. The quiet was broken only by the hiss of the fire and the bubbling of the cauldron.

Borekarek slowly lowered his hands and fixed Holly with a piercing stare. She flinched and lowered her eyes.

"I . . . I don't understand anything you said," she muttered.

"No, of course not. That is the nature of prophecies. But Korak left us the clues, and placed his pots outside of time to be found by the chosen one. This much we know."

Holly looked up quickly. "The pots? You mean the ones I've broken?"

Borekarek nodded. "I understand little of this and can explain less, but I will try. Korak was the greatest of our sorcerers. He was so powerful that he was able to work with time as a potter works with clay or as a weaver shapes fabric. He foresaw the trials that were to come and sealed some of those fragments of time in clay pots. These pots he placed outside of time to be kept safe until the Maregi should be drawn to them and break them. By releasing the time within them, the Maregi would travel through time and come to us in those chosen moments. When the time contained in each vessel ran out, the Maregi would leave us."

Holly was silent for a long moment. "So that's why I went back so suddenly. . . . I have no control over when I get here or when I leave," she said at last, feeling queasy.

"That appears to be true," agreed Borekarek, scratching his tangled beard.

"And where I am now, here. Is this a different world or a different time?"

"A different time, long before yours. We are the ancestors of many of your people. Our language is different from yours, but as you have noticed, you can understand us and we can understand you. This too is a sign that you are the Maregi."

"I still don't believe it." Holly's heart was pounding. "But even supposing I *was* this Maregi, what would I do?"

"I do not know."

"What!"

Borekarek smiled. "It is just as I said. Only the Maregi knows what the Maregi must do. The prophecy is a guide. We believe that it means our enemies will be defeated, but we do not know how."

"Well, if you don't know, how can I? That proves I'm not the Maregi—I haven't got a clue what to do." Holly felt a stab of relief.

"Think, my child." Borekarek moved closer, reached out and cupped Holly's face in his clawed hands. He looked deep into her eyes. "You have strengths that you have never dreamed of. The power is yours, inside you. You have only to recognize it and to call it forth."

She shivered. Dad had said something just like that before she left Vancouver with Mum.

"How—how do I do that?"

"It will become clear to you. Perhaps in your time, perhaps here. This is a dangerous time for us. Already this past midwinter we have seen the moon swallowed once. This will happen again three nights from now, at midsummer, and I believe that Maregi's power against the invaders will reach its fullness at this time."

Shouts from outside interrupted him. Borekarek's hands fell away from Holly's face and she turned with the others towards the doorway.

"Borekarek! Borekarek, Evaken!" called urgent men's voices outside. Evaken ran to the door and flung aside the skin. Avartha darted out after him, and Borekarek shuffled as quickly as he could towards the doorway. Holly followed, heart pounding. *There was fear in those voices.*

A knot of men stood outside, talking all at once. Holly

stood blinking once more at the painful change in light. At first all she could see was a collection of bodies in short, dark tunics. Then she noticed something else.

On the grass lay three men. Two were moaning in pain. Holly bit her lip as she noted an arrow protruding from the knee of one of them. The third man lay very still.

The others were shouting at Evaken and Borekarek. One of them gestured to a man kneeling on the grass with his arms behind his back. He was glaring defiantly at everyone. Instead of the dark tunic that flapped around the knees, this man wore a pair of trousers and a loose plaid shirt. His long hair was a brilliant red and was tied back with a leather thong. A collar of gold around his neck flashed in the sun. He seemed unable to move, and Holly realized that he was a captive.

"These stinking vermin leaped out of the rushes . . ."

". . . saved half the family . . ."

". . . Coran and Agad were sorely wounded . . ."

". . . set fire to the storehouses . . ."

The voices rose in a hopeless tangle. Holly edged away a little, then froze.

On the grass beside one of the wounded men was something very short with dark wavy hair. Something with huge, staring, bulging eyes. The man speaking in the loudest voice gestured towards it, and Holly gulped in horror. It was the bleeding, severed head of a man.

Avartha's voice wailed in grief. Evaken's face went white.

"This foreign viper," said one of the men through clenched teeth, "already had Rikka's head when Coran leaped on him from behind. Poor Coran got a dagger in the chest for it, but I got the weasel when he was down, and here he is! I should have killed him right then, but Ikar persuaded me that a captive could be useful."

Holly was shaking. She'd been to horror movies before with her best friend Sarah, but you always knew the blood was fake. This was real! Her stomach lurched, and suddenly she was leaning against the wall of Borekarek's hut, violently throwing up her lunch.

"Avartha!" Evaken shouted, "Take her away from here!"

Strong hands grasped her around the shoulders and some-one wiped her mouth with a rough cloth. She was shaking all over.

"Come, Hhollee," said Avartha's strong voice. "You must leave here. Borekarek is a healer; he will do what he can for the wounded men."

Shaking, Holly put one foot in front of the other and with Avartha's help managed to walk past the stone circle and down the slope. The voices faded. As they started slowly down the path by the stream, a cool wind ruffled her damp hair.

"Here, sit by the stream." Avartha steered her towards a tumble of rocks beside the water, and Holly sank thankfully down, still shaking. Avartha sat close by. The soft chatter of the brook filled the air and drowned out the sounds of voices on the hill.

"They are cruel people," said Avartha softly. "They cut off the heads of their enemies and keep them as trophies. They do not spare women and children, not even tiny babes. That is why we must stop them."

Holly drew a deep breath of sweet summer air. Below them the plains stretched away in a shimmering sea, peaceful and calm. *But that head!*

"You have not seen death before?"

Holly shook her head. "Not up close. There are pictures in the newspapers, and on TV—but you wouldn't know what I mean. . . ."

"Do people not kill each other in your time?"

"Oh, sure they do. But it's usually far away—not right in front of you, like this." She shuddered. All she could see was the man's bulging eyes. "Ugh!" she said, clenching her teeth. "I can't stop thinking about it!"

Avartha shook her head. "We have seen so much bloodshed this season past that I have grown accustomed to seeing dead and wounded men. I fear for my people. We have lost many good warriors."

Holly shifted on the rock and felt a lump in her right pocket. She reached in her hand and pulled it out. The raven brooch.

"Avartha," she said, unwrapping the tissue and holding it out in her palm. "Here. This is for you. You gave me the amulet; I want to give you this."

Avartha took the brooch and held it in her hand. "It is beautiful, Hhollee! Your artisans are powerful!"

"If you rub it with something to clean it, it'll get shiny."

Avartha rubbed the surface on her cloak, and smiled as the bird's belly began to glow.

"Thank you, Hhollee. It is a great treasure. I will keep it always!"

Holly looked down at the water beside her. "It doesn't have any magic protection to it, though. It's just an ordinary brooch."

"Even ordinary things can have power for those who give and receive. I thank you." Avartha stood up and glanced up at the sun. She extended a hand to Holly. "It is nearly time for the milking. I must return home."

Avartha walked quickly along the path, and Holly forced her shaky legs to keep up. The sick feeling had passed, but she had to stare intently at everything around her to stop seeing that head in her mind. When they finally reached the yard, Holly could hear a goat bleating from one of the grassy fields beyond the buildings.

But she also heard something else. A woman screaming.

"What?" hissed Avartha, running up the last hillock on the path.

They both halted and stared. Men on horseback were milling about the yard. They were shouting and laughing as the horses whinnied and danced impatiently. One of the riders had a large bundle slung over his horse in front of him; it was flailing arms and legs and screaming.

"Mama!" shouted Avartha, bounding forward.

"No!" Instinctively Holly grabbed Avartha's cloak and yanked her back with all her strength. "Don't! They'll get you too!"

"But I cannot let them take her! I—"

"What can you do?" hissed Holly, hanging on desperately. "They'll take you too!"

The man with Avartha's mother let out a wild whoop, spun his horse, and galloped out of the yard. The others whooped and followed him. The last one tossed a large, smoking stick at the thatch roof of one of the outbuildings and flames leaped up from it.

"No!" Avartha pulled away from Holly's grasp and ran for the house. The riders were not yet out of sight, and Avartha screamed after them.

"Mama! Let her go! Mama!"

But the smoke billowing out from the burning building soon filled the yard and obscured the retreating riders. The flames roared as the dry thatch caught fire.

"The storehouse!" cried Avartha, suddenly turning towards the fire. She bounded towards it.

"Are you crazy?" shrieked Holly, running after her and grabbing her cloak again. "You'll be killed! Look at it! It's too far gone!"

As she spoke the thatch collapsed in a shower of sparks and the flaming roof caved in. Holly yanked Avartha back, and the two girls landed sprawling on the packed earth of the yard as great tongues of flame darted out of the ruined doorway. Holly gasped for breath, then gritted her teeth as she realized her ears were buzzing.

"No!" she cried. "I can't leave now! I have to stay and help Avartha!"

But it was no use. She watched her feet dissolve in the air beside Avartha as the other girl's wails of grief faded into darkness.

CHAPTER SEVEN

THE LIBRARY

"AVARTHA!"

Holly beat her fists against the stone floor in helpless rage. Why did the time in the pot have to run out so soon? Avartha needed her! What if the men came back and captured her too? What if she was stupid enough to run after them?

She sat up, panting. The dim, flickering light of the flashlight she'd left on illuminated the two pots still on the shelf.

I could just go back right now! she thought excitedly. *I will! Avartha, I'm coming!* She lurched to her knees and reached out, then stopped.

Go back to where, to which moment? If what Borekarek had said was true, she had no control over which pieces of time she entered. She gritted her teeth in frustration and sank back on her heels.

Slowly her anger and panic trickled away as she recalled everything that had happened. She saw again the leaping flames and the billowing smoke . . . and that *awful* head. Holly shuddered.

Slowly, a gnawing relief crept over her. Holly shook her head. What was she thinking? She could have been hurt too! She could have been killed!

She sat there for a long time, weary and shaken. "I'm safe now! I'm safe!" she told herself over and over, chanting the words out loud. The sound of her own voice was comforting.

At last she grabbed the flashlight and pushed herself up unsteadily. Her hand touched something cool and smooth on the floor. Her recorder. She reached for it and held it a moment, enjoying its calm weight in her palm.

I'm never going back.

Without glancing back she pulled the heavy door closed behind her. Her foot struck something hard, and she stopped short. The other recorder!

She bent and ran a finger along its pale surface. Someone else had dropped it here. Who? How long ago? And why, why had that person dropped it here? Strange . . . as if the music had called someone else too, someone who turned in panic and ran, just like she had. . . .

She held it up beside her own black instrument. Light and dark, side by side. Who else in the family had been into music? Maybe Granny? She'd have to ask.

Holly lingered a moment in the outer doorway. How long had she been in there? Only a couple of minutes? It seemed like a lifetime. She stepped out into the bright sunlight and blinked, dazed. How could she act normal, after all that?

"Holly!" Aunt Sally was hurrying across the yard. "Your dad's on the phone for you!"

Dad! Holly broke into a run and blew through the house like a hurricane. She grabbed the old phone in the front hall.

"Dad!"

"Hey, Piper! I thought I'd try to get you after Mum left to keep those blues at bay. She's on her way then, I guess?"

"Yeah . . . left about—well, a little while ago. . . ." Holly panted, realizing that the whole afternoon was a blur now. How long *had* she been in that barn?

"Just wanted you to know that we both love you. Everything's going to be fine, I'm sure. And you're going to be fine too."

"I just wish you could be here, Dad!"

"I know, I know. I do too. But I have a feeling you're going to have some great adventures over there."

"Yeah, well . . ." She shivered, seeing again that terrible head. This was probably not the kind of adventure he had in mind.

"Did you make it out to Stonehenge yet?"

"Yeah . . . yesterday. But it was awful. They've built a stupid fence around it, and—well, get Mum to tell you about it."

"A fence! They always do that kind of thing, don't they. Bureaucrats."

"Dad . . ." Holly took a deep breath. There was so much to say—but how? *Please, please don't get a divorce! Let me hop the first plane home! And by the way, do you believe in time travel?*

"Yes?"

"I—I love you, Dad."

"I love you too, Piper. Listen, don't worry about a thing. You've already got the cell phone number, and I'm going to give you the number at the resort too so you can call us, day or night. Got a pen?"

"Uh, yeah." Holly stuffed a recorder into each back pocket, grabbed an old pencil and scrawled the number down on the note pad by the phone.

"You be sure to call if you need us, okay? Even if you just need to talk."

"Okay."

"Promise?"

"I promise."

"Good. I'll call again in a couple of days when we're settled in and Mum's over her jet lag."

"Okay." *My last chance to say something!*

"Okay, you try and enjoy yourself, sweetie. I'll talk to you again soon."

"Bye, Dad," she whispered, eyes closed. No other words would come.

"Bye, bye, Piper. I love you."

She hung up and stood staring at the ancient black phone, fighting back tears. Only Dad called her Piper, a name Mum hated. As a kid she had loved the story of the Pied Piper, but Mum thought the Pied Piper was evil because he took all the children away from their parents. Back then, all Holly could think of was what a wonderful, magical place they were going to deep inside the mountain. Today, she wasn't so sure.

"Cup o' tea for you, love? Oh!"

Holly whirled to see Aunt Sally lurching to a halt. A jet of hot tea splashed onto the faded mat in the hall.

"Aunt Sally! Are you okay?" She started forward, then stopped.

Aunt Sally was staring at Holly's left rear pocket, at the old recorder sticking out of it.

"Cor!" she said softly. "Where did you find that old thing?"

"In . . . in the barn," Holly said sheepishly. "I'm sorry, I know I'm not supposed to . . ."

Aunt Sally shook her head and chuckled. "Never mind that now, pet. Your Mum's a bit of a worrywart. I'm not bothered. But where was it? It's been lost for donkey's years."

"It was on the floor in the old passageway."

Aunt Sally took it from her and turned it over and over. "Gillian's recorder. I never . . ."

71

"Gillian? You mean Mum?"

"That's right, yes."

"Mum played the recorder?" Holly stared at her.

"Oh, yes. Played the flute too, and the oboe. Very serious about it she was, for years. Wanted to go on to music school, she said."

"What! She never told me that!"

"Not surprising, really. She gave it up all of a sudden. Mystified the lot of us. One day she was our old Gillian, and the next day she suddenly had a queer, wild look on her. Said she'd lost the recorder in the river while walking with her boyfriend, but that never sounded right to me. Gillian was never careless like that. Next thing we knew, she was on her way to Canada."

Holly was speechless. She tried to imagine Mum playing music but simply couldn't. And she'd never shown any interest in Dad's concerts, at least that Holly could remember. In fact, in the last couple of years, the more Holly got into playing music, the angrier Mum had become.

Aunt Sally was shaking her head and chuckling. "Daft of me to take such a turn. But it was a shock. I'll just get a cloth." She bustled back into the kitchen with her dripping cup and saucer.

As Holly helped her wipe up the mess, she wondered if underneath Aunt Sally's cheerful bluster there was something else, something like . . . uneasiness?

Holly followed her into the kitchen and took a deep breath. "Aunt Sally," she said, "tell me about my mum. Please."

Aunt Sally wrung out the cloth in the sink and turned. She gave Holly a crooked smile. "Right, love. It's time you saw the family albums."

72

And as she sat beside Aunt Sally at the kitchen table, gazing at one picture after another of Mum as a girl, Holly thought she'd entered a world even more surprising than Avartha's. This was England in the 1960s and 1970s, glaring at her from grainy black-and-white and garish colour photos—snaps as Aunt Sally called them. Mum and Aunt Sally in their school uniforms, arms linked and grinning for the camera. Mum in the old tree swing, hair flying, mouth open wide in a scream of delight—a version of Mum that Holly had never seen before. And Mum in a royal blue gown, poised and smiling, a silver flute gleaming in her hand.

"That was taken the night of her recital, just after she passed her exams," said Aunt Sally, pointing.

Holly leaned back, head swimming. This Mum was a complete stranger to her. Why had all of this been kept a secret?

"You look so like your Mum, Holly," sighed Aunt Sally. "At least the way she looked here . . ."

Holly wasn't really listening. "Does Dad know any of this? I mean, about the music?"

"Tell you the truth, love, I've no idea," said Aunt Sally. "In the early days I reckoned she fancied your Dad because he was musical. And perhaps that was true then. But now, from some things she's said the past couple o' weeks, I'm not so sure."

Holly's stomach knotted suddenly. "What . . . what do you mean?"

"That's not to say—don't misunderstand me now, love. . . ." Holly saw Aunt Sally's cheeks flush, saw her struggling for words. "What I mean is, you'd think she'd never lived any of this life here." Her finger stabbed at the photo of Mum with her flute. "You'd think she'd been born in Canada. It's as if she wants to forget. . . . There now, I've probably said too much. . . ."

"But just tell me—"

73

Uncle Ian burst through the back door with a huge container of take-out food in his hand.

"Picked up some curry at the chippy," he grinned. "There's enough for all!"

Holly bit her lip. She glanced at the kitchen clock and realized with a start that it was well after five. Uncle Ian had been gone for four hours. Mum would be boarding her plane soon.

Frederick slouched through the back door as if reeled in by the aroma of food and headed for the cupboard where the plates were kept. Holly had never seen him move so fast. And he was actually smiling.

"What's all this, Frederick?" teased Aunt Sally, rumpling his hair on her way to the sink. "One good meal a day not enough for you?"

"He's a growin' boy," protested Uncle Ian, dishing out the steaming curry. "Always one more corner left, i'nt that right, old lad?"

Holly watched the three of them grinning at each other, winced and turned back to the pictures of Mum. Surely she hadn't always been tense and grumpy. Had she? No. The smell of curry brought back memories of Sunday night dinners with Mum and Dad at the Raga Indian Restaurant down the street. They'd gone there almost every week for a while. Mum used to laugh a lot then. How old had Holly been? Eight, maybe nine? Suddenly she wanted desperately to phone Dad back, tell him about the recorder, tell him everything. . . .

"Some curry, Holly?" asked Uncle Ian, handing her a steaming plateful.

"Uh . . . sure. Thanks."

Without a word, Aunt Sally gently lifted the photo albums off the table and set out four sky-blue place-mats. The family history lesson was over, at least for now.

"WHAT SAY we go up to London one day, Holly?" said Aunt Sally as they scraped the last bits of curry from their plates.

"That would be fun," Holly said, not sure if it would or not. She and Mum had spent their first three days in England in a London bed and breakfast place full of loud tourists. She remembered crowds, diesel fumes, and double-decker buses.

"You didn't get a chance to see it properly before. We'll go to the zoo and the Tower of London, where Henry the Eighth beheaded his wives."

Holly swallowed hard. The beheading she could do without, but she wouldn't mind seeing the zoo.

"We can also take a trip out to the old Roman ruins at Bath if you like. Not all on the same day, of course!"

"Sure, that would be great," said Holly. *I know what she's up to,* she thought. Grown-ups always did this. They thought that keeping you busy would somehow make you forget all the awful things in your life. Her best friend Sarah's parents did this when they first broke up. Her dad took her on a whirlwind tour of the Aquarium, the Planetarium, and the Museum of Anthropology all in the same weekend. Sarah was so exhausted she got the flu.

"Right, then! I'll check the train times to London and we can make some plans." Aunt Sally rose and swept the plates off the table.

She was the old Aunt Sally again, brisk and jolly and determinedly cheerful. But she'd been different for a while this afternoon, when they were alone. . . .

Holly got up. "Can I help with the dishes, Aunt Sally?"

The sink was already full of soap bubbles. "No, love, you go on and relax. You look knackered. You've had a hard couple of days, I reckon. Go on with you now, I'll do the washing up."

Holly smiled gratefully and headed for her room. She closed

the door and looked around her. It was so empty with Mum gone. With an angry grunt she heaved her suitcase up onto the second bed. There. Now it didn't look quite so lonely.

A wave of exhaustion washed over her. She was too tired to be angry anymore. It was too much, too much. Too many things all at once . . .

She collapsed on her bed and suddenly felt the weight of the amulet. She laid a hand on her shirt, felt its shape underneath the fabric. The memories flooded back. A man had been killed and beheaded, and others had been wounded. She had seen blood, heard screams of pain. And then Avartha's mother had been carried off by those guys on horses! Would they kill her too? And what about that bruise on Avartha's face—didn't that make it all even more complicated? *Don't even think about it!* she told herself. *Forget it, just forget it!*

But she couldn't forget it—any of it.

She stood up and yanked the amulet out of the neck of her shirt. It gleamed like dark water. Suddenly, it felt like a noose, or a chain that bound her to that other world.

She had to get this thing off! She picked at the knot in the amulet's leather cord. It was no use. She tried to pull it off over her head but the cord was too short and she almost ripped her nose off. Finally she looked for some scissors. All she had was nail scissors, and they were too flimsy. The leather seemed indestructible. She scowled and tried again to pull the knot apart. No use. She stamped her foot, but accepted defeat for now. *I'm just too tired,* she thought. *Tomorrow I'll ask Aunt Sally for a pair of real scissors. Then I'll throw this thing somewhere where it'll be lost forever.*

As she crawled into bed, she noticed the two recorders on the quilt where she had tossed them earlier. She ran her fingers once again along the sleek, ivory side of the one that had been Mum's so long ago. She smiled and held it tight as she sank back into the pillows. It was important, somehow. The key to a secret. Maybe the key to a lot of things . . .

As the sweet summer dusk settled over the house, Holly fell asleep to the singing of distant frogs. There were no black wings tonight. She dreamed instead of Mum, swinging high between green leaves and blue sky, laughing.

"I HAVE TO GO into Salisbury for a meeting," said Aunt Sally the next morning. "Just for the morning. Would you like me to drop you off in the village? We've a small library there, and I'm sure Mrs. Witcher would let you take out some books if you like."

"A library?"

"Yes," smiled Aunt Sally. "It's very small, but they've a good collection all the same."

"Sure."

Holly stared out the car window in delight as lush fields bordered by overgrown stone fences whizzed by. This was the green and peaceful England she had always imagined. After a few twists in the road a cluster of shops and houses came into view. Aunt Sally pulled up in front of a very old-looking house with leaded glass windows and pink roses climbing up white-washed walls.

"Here we are," she said. "I'll come round to collect you about noon on my way back. If you'd like to leave earlier, just walk straight on along this road. It's only a couple of miles back to the house. All right?"

"Yes, fine," said Holly, climbing out. "Thanks very much."

The car roared off, and Holly pulled open the heavy old door. A pair of stone steps led down into the main part of the library. It was dim and cool and quiet here. Almost too quiet.

In the corner behind an oversized desk sat a frail old woman with a fog of white hair. Holly walked up to her, holding out Aunt Sally's letter.

"Mrs. Witcher? I'm Holly Gaynes."

The old woman fixed her with a pair of bright, ageless blue eyes. She opened the letter and read it.

"Right," she said in a shaky voice. "But I can only let you have two books the first time, love. That's the rule. Next time you can take out more."

"That's fine," said Holly. She turned away quickly and headed for the books.

The shelves here were strange. The libraries at home had metal shelves, but these were made of wood—dark, carved wood unlike anything she had ever seen. Holly let her finger trail along the edge of one shelf as she moved between two rows of books. The tip of her finger began to tingle, and she drew it back suddenly.

She came to the end of the row and stopped to gaze at the end of the bookshelf. Here the wood was carved in even more intricate patterns, an interlace of leaves and twisted branches. She laid her hand on it, and this time she felt a shock flow through her, as if the wood were still rooted and growing and the life of the tree had flowed into her body.

Holly snatched her hand away. *What kind of library is this?*

She deliberately turned away and scanned the small handwritten signs on the shelf ends for the fiction section. At last she found it and chose two detective novels, one pirate adventure and one of those teen romances Sarah was always reading. She'd have to pick two.

It was only a few minutes after ten o'clock. Holly stood uneasily, wanting to stay and read, yet troubled by those strange wooden shelves. *Don't be so stupid!* she scolded herself.

Your imagination is just working overtime. A couple of faded armchairs beckoned from the opposite corner. She squared her shoulders and headed towards them.

She stopped still when she reached them. A round wooden coffee-table stood between the two chairs, and on it lay a large book called *Stonehenge and Astronomy.*

She glanced around the library in panic. No other books lay around waiting to be reshelved. Only this one. Waiting for her.

Idiot! she told herself angrily. *That doesn't mean you have to read it!* She edged past the table and sat down in one of the chairs. She set three of her books on top of the large volume and opened a detective novel.

Holly tried to focus on the page but soon realized she was reading the same sentence over and over. She threw the book down in exasperation and picked up the romance. It was the same. She rubbed her eyes savagely. What was wrong with her?

She closed the romance and glared at the large book on the table. *Forget it!* she raged silently. *I'm not going to read a book I don't want to read!* She crossed her legs and crossed her arms in front of her chest and sat silent and fuming.

This was, of course, very boring. With a growl she lifted the paperbacks onto the floor and opened the cover of the large volume. *All right, just one look!*

The book was full of diagrams of Stonehenge with marks pointing out the spots of various sunrises and sunsets in relation to the stones. The writing was hard to understand, but the pictures and diagrams weren't so bad. The basic idea seemed to be much the same as what Dad had said. Stonehenge was some kind of huge dial that kept track of the movements of the sun and moon. One chapter was called

"Eclipses." She flipped through it, understanding little except that a series of small pits at Stonehenge could have been used to predict eclipses of the moon. She closed the book as a phrase glided through her mind: "When night eats the moon." If you didn't know what an eclipse really was, wouldn't it seem like the night was eating the moon? And hadn't Borekarek said something about the moon being swallowed at midsummer?

But who cares? She pushed the book away and picked up the two detective novels. *I'm not going back, do you hear me?* she shouted silently at the book. She rose and walked towards Mrs. Witcher.

It wasn't even eleven o'clock, but she didn't want to stay in here any longer. Why not walk back to the house? It was only a couple of miles, and the sun was even shining for once. Holly climbed the steps and swung the door open.

A gust of wind caught her and almost knocked her off her feet. She struggled to push the library door shut behind her. Stray leaves and newspapers were whirling through the air. Holly fought to keep her flying hair out of her eyes. The sky had darkened overhead, and thunder rumbled in the distance. *I knew that sunshine was too good to be true!* she grumbled to herself. She hesitated. Should she stay and wait out the storm?

"Awk!" came a sound from in front of her.

She looked down. A big black crow stood there, blocking her way. A raven.

"Shoo!" she cried, waving her free arm at it. It didn't move. It stood there, feet planted apart, bright eyes glittering at her.

She tried to squeeze around it. She stepped to the left, then to the right, but it matched her every move. She stopped, feeling trapped. Its sharp black eyes glittered.

"Awk!" it croaked. "Maregi!"

"What!" Holly gasped.

"Maregi! *Awk!*"

Had she heard it say 'Maregi'?

"I am *not* Maregi!" she yelled.

"Maregi!" rasped the bird again. Then as Holly watched in disbelief, the edges of the crow began to blur. Its shape became smoky and indistinct as it rose and grew into the watery figure of a cloaked old man. But the bright eyes remained the same.

"Maregi!" he said in a very human voice.

Holly blinked, heart pounding. Was this a hallucination? A violent gust of wind buffeted her.

"Who are you?" she choked out.

The crinkled face before her smiled but did not answer. Then suddenly the man began to shrink again. In a moment he was a crow once more—a crow that cocked its head at her and winked one beady eye, then rose in the air and flew away. The wind died abruptly.

Numb and drained, Holly pulled her fingers through her tangled hair and stared at the spot where the bird had stood.

A car horn tooted beside her. She jumped and turned to see Aunt Sally pulling up in front of her. She yanked the door open in relief and tumbled in.

"I'm early," said Aunt Sally, "but I see you found something to read."

"Glad you came along!" Holly gasped, still trying to untangle her hair. "That wind was incredible!"

"What wind, love?"

"That storm! I—" Holly stopped short and stared at Aunt Sally's puzzled face. The sun was blazing outside. The sky was cloudless.

Holly suddenly felt very cold. *Maybe I'm going crazy,* she thought.

"Never mind," she said, sinking down in the seat.

Aunt Sally shot her a sidelong glance. "Y'awright, then? You look like you've seen a ghost!"

"I'm okay, really. It was just a gust of wind."

"Was old Mrs. Witcher talking to her invisible folk again, then? She does that. I've heard her myself a few times when she forgot I was browsing. Very disconcerting, that is."

"No," said Holly, scowling. "Forget it. It was the wind."

"Tell you what, love, why don't we have a cup o' tea at the café. They serve a lovely cream tea."

"Uh, okay." Holly fixed her eyes on the dashboard as Aunt Sally pulled out into traffic.

Oh, great, she thought a moment later. The blue sign over the café door said The Raven's Nest.

CHAPTER EIGHT
SECRETS

"THIS IS A NICE LITTLE CAFÉ," SAID AUNT Sally, leading the way through the door. Inside, the air smelled of home baking— bread and buns and sweet things. Holly inhaled deeply, then coughed as she saw the murals.

They covered all but one wall, huge paintings of Stonehenge at different times of day—at sunset, by moonlight—and crowded with white-robed Druids, with a few cloaked, sword-wielding maidens thrown in for effect. Holly had to smile. The Druids were wrong, but the girls with swords were not so far from her own fantasies of . . . how long ago? Was it only days?

The place was almost empty. Aunt Sally led her to a table by an open window. Outside, birds hopped along the branches of a large tree, chirping merrily in the sunshine. So normal, so peaceful. Or were they? Holly chewed her lip. Was anything what it seemed?

"'Allo, Liz," Aunt Sally was saying to the smiling waitress. "Two cream teas, please."

"Right you are, then." The woman whirled away and reappeared a few moments later with a heavily laden tray. There were two cups and a large teapot, a couple of plates piled high with scones, and three stubby earthenware pots. Holly gasped as the waitress set the pots down in front of her. They looked exactly like the pots in the secret room. Korak's pots.

"Ye been down to the museum, then?" said the waitress, cocking her head at Holly. "Boss makes 'em—tries to make 'em look like them prehistoric ones in Salisbury museum, she says. Tourists like 'em. She's done a lot o' research, she has. She sells a few, if you're interested."

"Uh, no thanks. . . ." Holly sat very still as the waitress bustled away. Aunt Sally shot her a sidelong glance and cut open a steaming scone.

"Go on, Holly," said Aunt Sally, lifting the lid off one of the pots. "Let's see, this one's butter; the others will be preserves and clotted cream."

Gingerly Holly touched one of the lids. No shocks, no tingles. She grasped the small clay knob in the centre and pulled gently. Unlike the lids on Korak's pots, these ones were not stuck on. She peered into the pot and saw only a froth of pale yellow-white cream.

As she slathered her scone with butter, then strawberry jam and cream, she fought back a grim smile. Whoever Korak was, and whatever he was trying to make her do, he certainly had a sense of humour.

"What do you think, love? Good enough?" smiled Aunt Sally, wiping a blob of cream from the corner of her mouth.

"Delicious," said Holly. "I've never had this before."

"An English delicacy. Further west it's called a Devonshire cream tea, but nowadays you find versions of it all over."

"It's great," Holly mumbled around another mouthful. Still, the brightness of the sunlit café and the warmth of the tea couldn't erase the memory of that crow. Her eyes drifted back to the murals.

"Thought a cup o' tea would do you good," said Aunt Sally, stirring her tea with concentration. "You were gone pale there in front of the library. I've only ever once before seen a girl with that look on her, and that was your Mum the day she came running out of the barn."

Holly's knife froze halfway to the butter pot. "What—what do you mean? Tell me. What happened?"

"Can't say exactly," said Aunt Sally, almost casually, not looking at her. "She'd been practising her flute or her recorder in the barn for weeks—said the sound was good in there. Probably the same reason you like it. Then one afternoon I was bringing the cows in—we kept a few dairy cows in those days—and I saw her come running out of the barn like she'd seen a ghost. Ran straight into the house, locked herself in our room. Mum knocked on the door, pleaded with her for more than an hour. Finally, she opened up for me, but she wouldn't say a word about what happened. Never did."

Aunt Sally carefully spread a glossy layer of cream on her scone. "Not long after that, she told us she was off to Canada with her boyfriend. Those were the days when everyone went off travelling with their rucksacks. Mum and Dad begged her to stay—she was only seventeen, after all. But her mind was made up. And I expect you know what Gillian's like, once her mind is made up."

Holly stared down at her scone, unseeing. The recorder left on the dusty floor of the passage. Mum running out, scared. Had Mum heard the music from the pots too?

She felt a warm hand on hers.

"Something's happened, love. I don't know what that something is, much less what it's got to do with pottery." She jerked her head towards the pots on the table. "And I don't know *where* it's happened, at home or here in the library. You

85

needn't tell me a thing. But I'm here to listen, if you should need me."

Holly looked up and met those clear blue eyes. She was seized with a sudden longing to tell Aunt Sally everything. It would be such a relief.

But can I trust her?

Holly sat there for a long moment, lips parted, poised to take that leap into thin air. But she couldn't. She just couldn't.

She glanced outside. A robin had hopped onto the windowsill and was peering in cautiously. Suddenly, he turned and flew away. *Not quite ready to jump through the open window and join us,* Holly thought. Smart bird.

She fingered her cup, aware of Aunt Sally's silence. Certainly Aunt Sally seemed easier to talk to since their chat over the family photos yesterday. But what had happened in the barn was too crazy, too preposterous.

Besides, *you never, ever tell the grown-ups.*

She reached for the jam pot.

"You've got it all wrong," she said, trying to ease the tightness out of her voice. "Nothing's happened."

Aunt Sally sipped her tea in silence for a minute, then turned back to Holly with a smile. "A ghost, then?" she asked in a low voice. "Don't you worry, love. England's chock-a-block with ghosts. I won't think you're barmy."

Holly sighed in sudden annoyance. A ghost. That much Aunt Sally would believe. But the truth—no, never.

"No. No ghost. I told you, there's nothing wrong." Suddenly, she felt cornered. She hated that.

"Well, then." Aunt Sally reached for the teapot. A few last spoonfuls dribbled out of the spout.

Holly watched her out of the corner of her eye. Aunt Sally set the teapot back down and fingered the glossy lid absently.

A new shadow crossed her face. She raised her eyes and gave Holly a long, measuring look.

"I don't suppose you can get up to much trouble about our little farm," she said slowly, "but . . . you're not in any danger, are you?"

"No." *Is that a lie? How do I know? But I'm not going back, remember! So I'm not in danger!* "No. Don't worry."

"Well, love, I'll not press you then." Aunt Sally sighed. "I only ask because you reminded me so much of your mum there, all white and frightened. If you need to talk, I'm happy to listen."

Holly sat silently, playing with her empty cup. There was nothing she could say. Nothing safe.

Aunt Sally wiped her hands briskly and got up to pay the bill. She was joking with the waitress when Holly joined her at the till.

Holly took a last look at the murals as she followed Aunt Sally to the door. The girl in the bright red cloak seemed to grin straight at her. Was it the slanting sunlight that made her teeth gleam as if she had just flicked her tongue across them? As she caught the door, Holly noticed with a shiver that the girl had a bird on her shoulder. A raven.

THE NEXT THREE DAYS were spent zooming around on trains and buses to London and Hampton Court and Bath. She and Aunt Sally were alone on these excursions; Frederick had absolutely refused to come. Much to Holly's relief, Aunt Sally never mentioned the conversation in the café. She was her old, brisk self, arranging tickets and shepherding Holly on and off trains, explaining English history to her and buying her tea. It felt wonderful to be too busy to think. Once in a while, as they drove through miles of fields full of wild poppies waving in the

wind, Holly could even manage to forget Mum and Dad and
Avartha and Borekarek and all the complications that went
with them. But each night as she undressed for bed, she saw
the amulet gleaming against her skin. Each night she resolved
to ask Aunt Sally for a pair of scissors. But she never did.

"I'VE ANOTHER MEETING this morning, I'm afraid," said Aunt
Sally at breakfast on the fourth day. "D'you suppose you could
amuse yourself 'round here? I should be back by dinner time—
or lunch time, as you call it."

"Sure," said Holly, chewing her second slice of cold toast.
This stuff grows on you, she reflected in surprise.

Aunt Sally drove off a half hour later. Uncle Ian was at work
at the car repair shop he managed in the village, and Frederick
was out in the back garage, tinkering with his old car as usual.
Holly had learned to stay out of his way, and clearly he was
careful to stay out of hers. Holly wandered around the empty
house uneasily, just looking at things. She had never been
alone in here before.

The front room of the old house was dim and small. Holly
stopped in front of the row of pictures on the mantel. There
was Granny and Granddad on their wedding day, looking
impossibly young and nothing like the rosy, apple-cheeked
grandparents she had met as a child. There were photos of
Aunt Sally and Uncle Ian, of Frederick as a baby (looking more
cheerful than usual), of an older Frederick on a beach, proudly holding up a fish. There was even one of Holly herself as a
grinning toddler. But the only photo of Mum was the one of
her and Aunt Sally as little girls.

Holly wandered back to the kitchen and poured herself a
tall glass of milk. She pulled out the family albums from the
cupboard and flipped through them again, stopping at the one

of Mum with her flute. She stood tall, smiling serenely in that elegant dress. Her recital, Aunt Sally had said.

Holly sat back, remembering the quiet voices that had pierced her fog of sleep.

"Dare I ask how much we'll be throwing away?"

"Burton's has a used Hanes for three thousand dollars. . . ."

"This music thing is getting out of hand!"

Dad had won that battle. On her thirteenth birthday, Holly had unwrapped a slender package, opened the case and gasped at the silver flute glowing inside.

"Dad!" she squealed.

She threw herself into his arms, and he picked her up and whirled her around the room. "Will this one do?" he laughed.

"Will it do? You bet!"

As he set her down Mum walked out into the kitchen to pour herself a cup of coffee. She hadn't said a word.

Now Holly shook her head at the memories. Why would Mum pretend she knew nothing about flutes? She knew that a good one would cost money. For that matter, what about Mum's flute? Why buy one when you could just pass on the old one? Where was it? Had she lost that too, like the recorder? Had she thrown it in the river? And why? Say Mum *had* heard the music from the pots—was that terrifying enough to make her give up something she loved?

The thought of her own flute nestled inside her luggage sent a sharp pain through Holly. She missed playing. And why shouldn't she play? She had the house to herself this morning. She could play inside, well away from the barn and whatever strange powers lurked there. She gulped down the last of the milk and hurried to the bedroom.

The flute was as beautiful as she remembered it. It shone as she gently lifted the sections out of the blue case and fit them together. Holly rummaged in her suitcase for the music she'd brought with her. There was no music stand, but she propped it on the top of the bookshelf by the window and started to play.

Her flute sounded even sweeter than she remembered. She ran through the first few bars. *This is fantastic!* she thought excitedly. *Such a rich, full sound . . . must be the acoustics in this room.* She stopped to savour the resonance of the sound and then froze.

The music didn't stop when she did: it echoed and re-echoed around the room, around Holly herself, inside and outside her head. She dropped her flute, clapped her hands to her ears and screamed. It didn't stop. It was the high, sweet music of the humming pots.

"Not in here! No! Not in here too!" she shouted, collapsing on her bed. She sobbed as the humming filled the world, then slowly faded—like the song of a singer who glides away into the distance—until it was a dull ringing in her ears.

Holly lay on the bed, panting, tears running down her face.

And suddenly, she understood.

This was it: the thing that could drive you crazy, so crazy you'd run away from the people you loved and try to find a place on the other side of the world where this wild, sweet, dangerous music couldn't follow you. And if it did, you'd tear your hair and throw away the thing that meant so much to you and try to forget it, try to forget everything and become somebody new.

Holly flung herself off the bed and ran down the hall and out the back door. Her feet hit the soft grass and kept on running. She ran as far and as fast as she could. Past the garage, past the barn, past the old orchard, past the overgrown pastures. The long, tangled grass snatched at her feet, but she stumbled on until she reached the highest point of the hill above the house. She halted, gasping, beside a tree. From one of its branches there hung an old swing. Mum's swing.

The ropes were frayed, the wooden seat mossy. Holly sat down on it carefully. The ropes creaked but held.

The ringing in her ears was almost gone. Almost. Had she outrun the power of the pots? No. Impossible. She closed her eyes and listened to the quiet—to the twitter of birds, to the *hush, hush* of the wind dancing through the grass. She swung slowly back and forth, back and forth. Had Mum done this too, one last time, before she left for good?

Mum had heard the music. Holly was sure of it now. The pots had called her just like they had called Holly. Had the old door swung open for Mum too? Had she broken any pots? Holly thought back to the first time she'd entered the room. She was sure there were no pieces of broken pottery on the floor then; they were only there the last time when Holly herself had already broken the first pot. So Mum had heard the music, had been haunted and terrified by it, but hadn't travelled into the past.

Had she taken the flute with her, just in case she could outrun the music's power? You'd think that the west coast of Canada would be far enough away from here. But if it had been, Mum would still be playing, and life would be very different. No. That flute was probably at the bottom of the Pacific Ocean, growing a nice crop of seaweed.

Holly opened her eyes and gazed across the patchwork of green fields. From here she could see Amesbury and beyond; if she squinted, she thought she could even see Stonehenge glinting in the sun. This place was linked to Stonehenge somehow. And so was she. How could she stay away? But how could she get up the nerve to go back?

She wanted desperately to phone Dad and tell him what

she'd found out. She wanted to beg for advice. The scrap of paper with the phone number of the resort scrawled on it was still scrunched up in her pocket. She could run back to the house and call right now. She could. But she knew she couldn't. Not yet.

No. She had things to finish. She had to go back to Avartha's world and do whatever she was supposed to do. And to get back there, she had to play some music and break another pot.

She jumped off the swing and walked back down the hill, relishing the wind that lifted her hair, wanting to hang onto this moment of peace.

As she rounded the corner of the garage, she almost bumped into Frederick.

"Oh! Sorry!"

"Sorry!"

They both stopped short and stepped back from each other.

Holly felt her face burning. 'I'm so sorry. I wasn't watching where I was going."

"Neither was I. Never mind." Frederick looked down at his hands; they were smudged with grease. His shirt pocket was stuffed with tools, and a leather belt around his waist bulged with more.

"I—I was just heading back to the house," Holly said lamely.

"I was just going to pop into the barn." He glanced at her quickly, then looked away again. "Lookin' for some scrap metal. Got to patch the floor of the old Morris."

"The barn?" Holly tried to hide her alarm.

"Yeah, Granddad used to keep some bits of scrap metal in there. I've found a piece or two before. Worth a look."

92

"Yeah . . . right," said Holly. "Well . . . good luck. I mean, I hope you find something."

"Yeah." Frederick hesitated a moment, then stepped around her and disappeared through the barn door.

Holly watched him in despair. *What do I do now? I can't get to the pots while he's in there rooting around! I'll just have to wait and watch for him to leave.*

She walked back to the house on shaky legs. She lingered a moment in the kitchen doorway. The clock on the wall said eleven. Aunt Sally wouldn't be home for at least an hour. She had to get in there before Aunt Sally came back!

Holly ran to her room and found her rain jacket. She scooped up her flute from the floor where she'd dropped it and held it a moment, savouring its cool weight in her hand, watching the light slide over its smooth surface. *I'll take the flute this time,* she decided. She fitted it back into the case and slid it into one of the jacket's inside pockets. Then she rummaged in her suitcase for some granola bars; she might need them. Instead, her hands found Dad's book about ancient Britain.

I don't have time for this! she scolded herself. Nevertheless, she flipped it open and found herself staring at the last chapter, "The Iron Age Celts." The chapter talked about Salisbury Plain under Celtic control. Holly stared at the pages. Avartha's people had *not* driven back the invaders. The Celts had won and stayed. That was history.

What could she do, then? Would Avartha and Borekarek be killed? Was there no hope?

Whatever happens, I have to be there!

Holly dropped the book and pulled the bedroom door shut. Then she ran down the hall.

Was Frederick still in that barn? She cracked open the door and listened. No sounds from the garage. From the back window in the kitchen with its lacy half-curtain Holly could watch the barn door without being seen from outside. Or so she hoped. She stood very still as the kitchen clock ticked the minutes away.

Eleven-fifteen. Eleven-thirty. Eleven-forty. *Come on! What are you doing in there?*

Maybe he came out long ago while I was reading that book. Holly had almost convinced herself of this when Frederick emerged from the barn with a long strip of metal. He glanced once at the house, and Holly shrank back against the cupboard on the far wall. Then he disappeared into the garage.

Holly let out a long breath. She tiptoed to the back door, which she'd left half open, and listened. Silence. Then a metallic creak. The whine of a power tool.

Go, girl! She slipped outside and ran for the barn. Nothing must stop her now.

Chapter Nine
The Enemy Camp

THE COOL CLAY POT ALMOST LEAPED OUT OF her hand. The hurricane tore at her hair and buffeted her to her knees, but she pulled her jacket around her and hunkered down. Then the storm died, and there was nothing but darkness.

Holly blinked. She couldn't see a thing. Still on her knees, she turned this way and that, searching for a pinprick of light, a shadow—anything. Had she gone blind? She smelled damp leaves, wet soil, a whiff of smoke. She reached out in front of her, and her hands touched prickly things. Her knees felt wet, and as she shifted her weight, a loud crack shattered the silence. A twig.

She felt around carefully with her hands. There were skinny branches and plenty of leaves. She tipped her head back and gazed upward. A ragged shadow above her leaned across a patch of starry sky. Maybe she was in one of those little clusters of trees and brush that dotted the plain. But why? And where was she supposed to go from here? She hadn't expected this.

Holly managed to lurch to her feet without losing her balance and took a step forward.

Crack, crack! went another fifty twigs. She changed direction and took a few cautious steps. There didn't seem to be as much underbrush here, and Holly walked slowly forward, arms outstretched.

She had been inching forward for what seemed hours when she caught a stronger whiff of smoke and stopped. Was that a faint glow ahead? As she peered into the gloom, she heard the spitting of a fire and voices, men's voices. Holly froze and held her breath. Friends or foes? She couldn't know unless she got close enough to see and hear them. Carefully, crouched and feeling the ground ahead with her fingers, Holly crept forward, one hand, one foot at a time.

Suddenly, she could see the campfire winking through the lattice of underbrush in front of her. She heard a loud guffaw. From the darkness on the left came the soft stamping and blowing noises of tethered horses. Holly crouched down to peer through the leafless lower stalks of the underbrush. She caught her breath as she saw a group of men with fiery hair in long ponytails. Most of them had long, droopy mustaches. They were dressed much like the hostage she'd seen at Borekarek's place, except that they all wore cloaks pinned at one shoulder. They looked like they'd just stepped out of that chapter on the Iron Age Celts.

These guys must be Celts!

They were sitting cross-legged on the ground in a circle around the fire. A whole pig was roasting on a spit over the leaping flames. The men were passing around a bulbous drinking skin. Firelight flashed on the gold ornaments around their necks, wrists, and fingers. Holly hadn't seen this much gold outside of a jewellery store.

"Two more nights!" said one man, wiping his mouth with the back of his hand and passing the skin to his neighbor.

"Do not be so sure," growled a man on the other side of the fire. He was facing Holly and looked older than the others. His face was set in a scowl. "The woman may be lying or not telling all. These dark little people are slippery as weasels. I do not trust them."

"Nonsense," said the first man. "She speaks the truth. I have heard from others that this is their most important festival. The people will not stay away."

"But I saw the carts going up to their hilltop fortress," protested another man whose back was towards Holly. "They were loaded down, as if the people were ready to stay for a long time."

"They must come out to worship their sky gods," insisted the first man. "It is the most important day of the year for them. And when they do come out, we will be ready."

Holly chewed her lip. They must be talking about midsummer, the day that Borekarek said was so important. They were planning an attack for that day! A sudden anger flared up in her. How unfair to attack a bunch of people in the midst of their religious ceremony. But it made sense. Dad had told her a bit about ancient war strategy. You had to make the most of your advantages. And surprise was certainly a big advantage.

She hoped she had heard correctly. For some reason, she had to listen very hard to understand these people; they sounded different from Avartha and Borekarek. She decided to listen carefully and learn as much about their plans as she could.

"They are not stupid, Boca," said the older man, glaring across the fire at his younger comrade. "We have burned every storehouse east of the river now. They know we will not turn around and sail back across the sea. They must be planning something."

"Well, ask the woman yourself. Perhaps your dagger is sharper than mine." Holly caught the flash of a grin and shivered.

When the older man merely grunted, Boca rose and walked out of the circle of firelight. He reappeared a moment later, dragging a reluctant cloaked figure with him. He threw her to the ground in front of the doubter. The hood slid back from her face and Holly's eyes widened. It was the mother of Avartha and Evaken.

She sat motionless at the older man's feet, her hands bound in front of her. His pale eyes studied her. Then he made a quick hand signal to one of the men near him and spoke.

"You say that your people's midsummer ritual is the day after tomorrow. True?" The man by the fire repeated the words to the woman.

"True." She stared at the ground in front of her as the same man repeated her answer. Holly realized with a start that these people could not understand the woman's language; they needed a translator.

"And all the people must attend?"

"Only the priests."

The man's eyes narrowed. "That is not what happened in past years."

"If our people are in danger, the priests do the rituals alone. And our people are certainly in danger." She looked up at him defiantly.

"What time of the day does the ritual take place?"

"At sunrise."

"Only at sunrise?"

There was a moment's pause. Holly could see a faint sheen of sweat on the woman's brow. "Yes."

The older man stepped in front of her and drew out a short sword. He held the point under her chin.

"If you lie . . ." His unfinished threat hung like a blade in the air as the man by the fire repeated the words calmly, automatically.

She held still, unflinching, eyes flashing at him. "I do not lie."

"We shall see. Take her away." One of the other men leaped up and led her back into the shadows.

"It will be a child's game, Ankios. You will see," drawled Boca, lazily sharpening his dagger on a small stone.

"Huh!" growled Ankios. "What do we gain by slaying their priests and not their warriors?"

"The warriors will come, be sure of that. Besides, without their priests these people will be like lost sheep. The whole land will be ours in no time. The land and all its riches."

"And if their warriors do *not* come to the stone circle, then we are faced with laying siege to their fortress for weeks on end."

The young man shrugged again. "Then we starve them out, however long it takes."

"Well, I for one would rather see a quick resolution," said the young translator. "A swift battle, their best warriors slain, and all the land and women ours. I have my eye on one dark beauty already." A big grin spread across his face.

"What, the woman's daughter?" asked Boca, eyebrows raised in mock surprise.

"Yes. A fine filly."

"Fine indeed; but you may have to fight me for her."

"You forget I outrank you, Boca."

"Idiots!" roared Ankios, standing up. "You sit here arguing over a woman as if we already owned this land! It may never be ours if we are not careful! We need a sound strategy!"

Holly was stiff from crouching. She *had* to get away from

here; she had to find Borekarek and warn him of the planned attack. But which way was Stonehenge? With dark trees and brush all around her, Holly had no sense of direction.

"Don't jump out of your skin, Ankios," drawled Boca. "Let Camanom and me go out there tonight to see what we can see."

"To their fort?"

"No, no, no. To the ring of stones." Boca waved one arm languidly in the air, indicating a direction to the right of where Holly was crouched. "We may overhear something useful."

"You do not know their language, you fool!" sneered Ankios.

Boca shrugged easily. "I have learned a few words. And Camanom is fluent."

Holly's heart was pounding. She had to get out of here now! She squinted at the ground in the direction from which she thought she had come. The dim glow of the firelight showed a faint, mossy path. Painfully she unfolded her cramped legs and tried to stand up. Her right foot was tingling. A small twig cracked under it as she put it down. She froze. A horse neighed in the darkness.

"What was that?" said Ankios sharply.

"A squirrel or a rabbit."

"No! A spy!" His voice was closer now. In panic, Holly made the only decision she could make. She turned and ran.

Branches exploded under and around her. Leafy fronds whipped her face. The path she had followed was still there, narrow but adequate, and she crashed on.

"After him! After him!" The men were all shouting at once now. She had to break free of this tangled underbrush!

She drove herself on through the noise and the pain,

becoming dimly aware of another sound just above her. It grew louder, hovered over her, then wheeled away towards the campfire. It was the beat of wings. The same wings that had thundered in her dreams.

She heard a yelp of fear. "Look! The gods preserve us!"

"It is Cathubodua!"

"Halt, you idiots!"

"An omen! The war goddess has come!"

Holly crashed on in the confusion, and in a moment the clinging underbrush fell away. She stumbled out onto the grassy plain and halted, panting painfully. To her left and behind her shone the small glow of the fire, barely visible behind the shelter of trees. The shouts continued. Holly had never heard such terror in people's voices before, and she shuddered. As she looked back, a black shadow disentangled itself from the darkness of the trees and dove towards her. One of its wings brushed her head before it turned and wheeled away; it swooped once more, as if to be sure of her attention, then sped off in the direction of the rising moon.

Holly shook her head in wonder and ran a hand through her hair. *The raven is a servant of the gods. She will protect you.* That's what Avartha had said. And yet Holly had spent so much time fearing the raven, dreading those dreams. The raven was her protector, not her enemy. The thought filled her with a sudden and unexpected joy. With a lightness of heart that surprised her, she sprang forward and broke into a run. She felt suddenly free, as free as the great bird soaring above in the moonlight.

And it wanted me to follow! She suddenly felt convinced of this. She turned to face the moon and ran towards it, sure that this was also the way to Stonehenge.

She breathed deeply of the sweet night air. The moon was

slung low in the sky ahead of her, huge and golden, rippling the dark plains with amber light. A cool breeze lifted her hair as she sped on over the soft grass. The amulet bounced out from under her T-shirt and thumped to the rhythm of her stride. Holly raised her face to the starry sky and let a rare wave of pure happiness wash over her.

This night is magical, and I am part of the magic! Holly felt calm and whole, as if she had become part of something vast and wonderful.

She ran for a long time over low hills and through little valleys. The moon climbed higher, and its light changed from gold to silver. It was so brilliant that she could see every hump and hollow in the ground. The air grew cooler, and a damp wind sprang up, singing in the grass that nodded in waves at her feet.

A sudden pang shot through her. Could this have been Mum instead, running here under the moon? If Mum had not turned away from the music all those years ago, would she have broken the pots? Would she have been the Maregi instead? But from what Borekarek had said, it sounded like there was only one Maregi.

At last she slowed. The ground rose ahead of her and she thought she glimpsed a flash of white. As she drew nearer and began to climb the gentle slope, she saw the stones in the moonlight. By the time she reached Stonehenge, her chest was heaving and her legs were wobbling uncontrollably. She barely noticed the radiant pillar stones, half white brilliance, half black shadow. She panted and gasped her way to the door of Borekarek's hut. A broad ribbon of light showed underneath the door-skin. Holly leaned on the doorpost, wiped the sweat from her streaming brow, and knocked.

She heard shuffling noises inside. A shadow fell across the

light under the skin as it was pulled back, and a hoary head poked out, glowing like angel hair in the moonlight.

"I'm back," panted Holly.

"Who? What?" the old man growled. At least he didn't have the bear-head on this time.

"It's me. Your Maregi."

"Ah!" He sucked in his breath with a whistling sound. "Come in! Come in!" He held the skin aside for her and she slipped past him into the warm hut. She shrugged off her jacket and stood sweltering in the dim light.

The fire was burning low. The huge cauldron had been removed from its usual hanger above the coals, and the soft light winked on rows of stone jars along one wall and ragged bundles of drying herbs hung from the ceiling. For once Holly could actually see properly in here. She glimpsed a yawning Evaken seated by a low shelf in one corner, fingering a carved stick.

"Well, young Maregi," rasped Borekarek, beckoning her to sit on a pile of skins by the fire. "Your time draws near."

"I know. It's midsummer soon, isn't it?"

Borekarek nodded gravely. "The day after tomorrow." He squinted at her. "You look tired, and . . ." he reached forward and gently touched her cheek, "you have been hurt. What has happened?"

Holly rubbed her face. "I fought my way out of some underbrush and ran across the plain. When I broke the pot this time I ended up a few miles from here. Some of your enemies had made camp there, and I heard them talking about their plans."

Borekarek's eyes grew wide. "You heard them? Do you mean that you understood them?"

"Well . . . yes," said Holly. "They sounded different from you, but I could understand them if I listened hard enough."

"Indeed!" Borekarek shook his head. "Korak's magic is more potent than I thought. The enchantment of the pots must allow you to understand both races. To us, their speech sounds like the babble of babes. But what did they say?"

"They were talking about attacking you here at sunrise on midsummer, when you are gathered for your ceremonies or whatever you do here."

Borekarek grunted in disgust. "I am not surprised. That is what we have been preparing for."

"They also had a woman prisoner, and I think she's Avartha and Evaken's mother." She looked at him uneasily. "They had someone translating what she said, and she told them that only the priests—I guess that means you and Evaken—will be here around the stones."

Borekarek smiled. "Clever woman, our Vedda. A lie which they are unlikely to believe, but worth the attempt nevertheless. No, Maregi, we must all be at this ritual, from babes to warriors. It is the most important festival of our year. This summer it is even more important, since the night before, the moon will be swallowed. Even if I could forbid the people to leave Sarum, they would not obey me. But tell me," he leaned forward, "did Vedda say anything of the night ceremony?"

"No."

"Good. They could surprise us more easily in the night, especially when the world darkens as the moon is eaten."

"They seemed suspicious, though, when she told them that the sunrise ceremony was the only one."

"Ah." Borekarek scratched his weedy beard. "Then we must be prepared for them to come by night."

"You'd better all have your swords or whatever with you. These guys looked dangerous."

"My dear young one," said the wizard, meeting her gaze,

"we have already armed everyone, even the women and older children. But know this: the more I study the rune-sticks, the more I believe that the answer lies in your hands. No amount of weapons will help us."

Holly gritted her teeth. "I told you before—I can't fight!"

Borekarek shook his head. "Fighting is not what is needed. Evaken! Bring the Salgren stick."

Holly glanced over at the bleary-eyed apprentice. He brought the slender piece of wood he was holding and sank down on the skins beside Holly. He placed it in her out-stretched palm.

Holly stared at it. It looked like the stick she had seen in his hands when they first met. Strange carved symbols crowded every available space on its surface. They wrapped themselves around the stick in a spiral, and Holly couldn't tell where they started and stopped. The marks were deeply carved, and their edges, polished by the touch of many hands, winked in the firelight.

"Show her," commanded Borekarek.

"See here," squeaked Evaken's changing voice as he pointed at the middle of the stick. Holly looked at the symbol. It didn't look like much of anything—just a short, straight line.

"That's it?" she asked.

"Indeed it is," Borekarek nodded gravely.

"But . . . is it supposed to mean something to me?" Holly frowned.

"It is the source of your power."

"But I don't know what it means! A lot of good that'll do me!"

"Think, my child." Borekarek leaned forward and touched Holly's forehead lightly. "It is something very important to you. Something you cannot live without."

Holly stared at him. "Well, food and water, of course—"

"No, no! These are needs which all people share. No, this is something else—something that is required for your spirit, not your body."

Holly looked down at the stick again, at that thin, straight line. And suddenly she became aware of a hard lump under her right knee in the pocket of her discarded jacket. She reached in and pulled the flute case out. She opened it and carefully fitted the pieces together.

Her flute gleamed like bright water in the firelight. A glowing line, thin and straight.

"Something I can't live without," she murmured. Mum had tried, oh, she had tried. But she hadn't quite managed it. Her soul was parched, starved for music.

"Maybe it's this," she said. "My music."

Borekarek and Evaken were both staring at the instrument.

"What is this thing?" Borekarek asked.

Holly didn't answer but put the flute to her lips and played "The Ash Grove," an old English folk-song that she'd always thought sounded particularly haunting on the flute. The other two stared at her as if enchanted. Clearly, they had never heard such music before.

"That is beautiful," said Borekarek. "It is a gift from the gods. This is indeed your power, Maregi."

"Maybe so," said Holly, cradling the flute in her hands, "but I've never seen music knock anyone sprawling, let alone kill. If this is going to help you against your enemies, there'll have to be some other magic involved too."

"If Korak's magic is powerful enough to bring you here, it is powerful enough to help you conquer. I have no doubt about that."

Holly stared at the light rippling through the glowing coals on the hearth. She wasn't so sure. A sliver of fear gnawed at her. If her music was *not* the answer, she was in a lot of danger. She might never get out of here alive. She remembered her panic back there in the woods, when she knew the Celts were after her. Then a memory nudged her. There was something else she had to tell Borekarek.

"I almost forgot!" she said. "The invaders were talking about sending a pair of spies out here tonight. I don't know if they'll do it now that the bird scared them all so much, but you should watch out."

"The bird? What bird?" Borekarek leaned very close.

"It was weird," she said, shivering as she remembered. "When I heard the men talking, I knew I had to tell you about their plans. But I made enough noise in the bush that they heard and started chasing me. I thought they'd catch me for sure, but then this big bird just—I don't know—flew out of nowhere! It flapped above me for a minute and then flew at the men. They were terrified. They kept shouting something about an omen from the war goddess."

"Indeed!" exclaimed Borekarek, his eyes suddenly gleaming. "That is very intriguing. You say they thought it was a war goddess?"

"Yeah . . . and a really bad omen. That's why I thought maybe they wouldn't come tonight."

"Still, we must be cautious. Evaken! Call Serak."

Evaken lurched up and ducked outside.

Borekarek's eyes were glowing. "This may be of great use to us. We know they have better weapons than ours, and those quick, horse-drawn carts allow them to attack swiftly. But if we know what they fear, we may perhaps use their fear against them."

Evaken reappeared, followed by a young man with both a long dagger and an axe slung at his hip.

"Serak, this is the Maregi," rumbled Borekarek. "She has overheard some enemy plans and warns us that there may be spies here tonight, here at the Circle. Be wary. Call Ketuk and Arag to watch with you."

Holly watched the young man. He was very good-looking, with sleek dark hair and black eyes. She noted a widening of these eyes at the mention of her overhearing the enemy, but otherwise he kept himself under perfect control. He stood straight and stiff and bowed slightly to Borekarek when the wizard had finished speaking.

"We will keep close watch, Borekarek," he said and bowed once more before turning on his heel and vanishing into the night outside.

"I am surprised that he did not stop you when you came up the hill," mumbled Borekarek to the fire. "He and his men have been watching over me lately. No matter. You must be thirsty, young Maregi, after your long run over the plains." He got up and shuffled over to a stone pot in one corner.

"Yes," Holly murmured, suddenly very tired. Carefully she fitted her flute back in its case. She braced herself against the mound of furs to keep from swaying.

"You must sleep here tonight," said Borekarek, ladling something out of the pot into a wooden bowl. "Tomorrow night will be a long one. You will need to rest."

"Yes," said Holly, sinking further into the skins. Then an anxious thought nudged at her. "Borekarek, where is Avartha? The last time I saw her . . . it was awful. Everything was on fire, and—"

"She is well. She has been staying in Sarum with the others." He set the bowl in her hands.

"Will I see her tomorrow?"

"She will be here to help with our preparations."

Holly set the bowl to her lips and drank deeply of the purest, sweetest water she had ever tasted. She handed it back to him. "Will the invaders kill her mother?"

"I do not know."

"She was so brave, even when they threatened her with a sword." As she spoke, Holly thought that drowsiness was overtaking her. Then she realized with a start that her ears were buzzing. Her eyes flew open and she gasped at Borekarek in panic.

"No! No, I can't leave now!" she cried. "Please, no! Don't let me go!"

But she was already dissolving in the warm air of the hut. The last thing she saw was Borekarek's alarmed face and the sight of Evaken stumbling towards him.

CHAPTER TEN
THE LAST POT

HOLLY SOBBED AS THE CLOSE AIR OF THE HUT evaporated and she felt the stone floor harden beneath her. She lay on the cool flagstones, letting the quietness of the room seep through her. Slowly she became aware of something cradled in her arms. The flute case.

She sat up. Why had she been wrenched away at that moment, just when things were really getting interesting? She glanced at the shelf on the wall. One pot left. One more cupful of time in which to accomplish . . . what?

She stood up. Why not go back right now? What was there to do here that was more important? She tried to remember the morning.

The music ringing in my ears, and Mum. The memories flooded back. Then with a start she remembered Aunt Sally. *How long was I gone?* She stumbled to the door and pulled it shut behind her. She stopped in the brighter light of the barn and looked down at her jeans. The knees were caked with dried dirt. Her running shoes were filthy and her T-shirt stained with mud. And where was her jacket? Probably still back in Borekarek's hut. She ran a finger down

110

her cheek. It still hurt. If Borekarek had noticed the scratches from those whiplike branches, so would everybody else.

What am I going to do? She hesitated at the doorway. She might be able to explain the scratch, but not the filthy clothes. *I have to get into the house before anybody sees me—now!*

She peered out the door. No sounds from the garage, but then that wasn't too unusual. Frederick seemed to spend hours in there doing nothing. And no red car in the driveway yet. Good. Aunt Sally wasn't home. Holly slipped through the door and ran.

And ran right into Frederick.

"Uh!" The impact knocked the wind out of her.

Frederick thrust the power tool he'd been carrying into his belt and grabbed her arm. "What's all this, then? What are you doing in there all the time? Snoopin' around like this, crawlin' about who knows where!" He pointed to her muddy knees. "Lookin' for family treasures to take home, are you?"

"Frederick, I can explain."

"Ye've been snoopin' around ever since the day you and your mum first got here!"

"No, I haven't!" Holly yanked her arm out of his grip. She stooped to pick up the flute case she'd dropped and angrily shoved it into the back of her jeans. "Why are you so mad, anyway? You're always mad!"

"Why'd you have to come here? We were goin' on holiday to Portugal before your mum rang up and ruined everything!"

"Well, pardon me, but you know I never wanted to stay here this summer! It wasn't my idea!"

They glared at each other, nose to nose, breathing hard. Holly realized she'd never really looked at Frederick before. His freckles stood out on his cheeks like pimples, but his blue eyes were her own mum's eyes.

"What *is* that bloody noise?" Frederick turned towards the barn door.

She noticed the music then. It was louder than she'd ever heard it, pouring out of the barn door like a flood.

"What've you done in here, then?" Frederick yelled at her, pushing past her and rushing into the barn.

"Frederick, no!" She bolted after him.

He was halfway down the old passageway when she caught up to him and grabbed his shirt, yanking him back with all her strength.

"Just slow down and listen to me!" she cried.

But he ignored her, and he was stronger than she was. He pushed on. The door to the pot room stood open, music tumbling out like a tidal wave. Frederick put his hands over his ears and looked inside.

"Nothin' but a bloody pot! What is this?" He stepped inside, reached over and picked up the pot. A wave of astonishment washed over his face.

"No! Give me that!" Holly sprang forward and snatched it away from him. "Don't touch it! You don't understand!"

"I understand it ain't yours! Now give it here!" He lunged forward and grabbed the pot.

"No!" Holly screamed, snatching at his hands.

Suddenly the pot flew away from both of them and shattered on the floor. Light and storm thundered through the room. She held her head down as the wind howled around them.

A moment later, Holly heard an astounded "Cor!" beside her as the broken shards on the barn floor melted into soft grass.

Holly raised her head as her stomach tied itself in a knot. *Oh, no! What am I going to do with him?*

THEY WERE BACK at Stonehenge, bathed in the golden light and lengthening shadows of a summer evening. Beside her Frederick lay sprawled on the grass as if he'd just been dropped from an airplane. He sat up and stared at the standing stones, open-mouthed.

"Where *are* we?" he choked out.

"The British Museum, stupid! Where do you think?"

"It's Stonehenge, isn't it?"

"Of course it is—only it's Stonehenge a long time ago, in prehistoric days! I told you not to touch that pot!"

The thunder of running feet interrupted her. A mob of young men with daggers and spears was rushing towards them.

"Stop!" she shouted in panic, scrambling to her feet. "It's me, the Maregi!"

Serak was in the lead. He skidded to a halt a couple of feet away, gesturing to the others. They stopped but did not lower their weapons. Serak studied Frederick with a long, stern stare. Frederick lurched to his feet, white-faced and speechless.

"I know *your* face, Maregi," said Serak, "But the youth with you is a fire-haired one, an enemy."

A fire-haired one. Holly stared at Frederick. Why hadn't she noticed it before? Frederick's red hair was the same colour as that of the Celts.

"No, no!" she said. She stepped to Frederick's side and took his arm without thinking. "You're wrong! He's not your enemy! Frederick is from my world. He's my cousin, my mother's sister's son. He's family."

The men glared at her.

"Then you come from a family of traitors, those who dare to marry the enemy!" growled one. The others murmured their assent and edged nearer, weapons raised, until both Holly and Frederick faced a forest of spear points.

Heart pounding, Holly glanced sideways at Frederick. His eyes were wide with terror. And with good reason.

I'm the only thing standing between him and death, she realized. And two minutes ago she'd been screaming at him! She took a deep breath and stepped right in front of Frederick. At the very least, she could shield him with her own body.

Aunt Sally's question echoed back to her: "You're not in any danger, are you?" And her answer: "No."

What a joke! Now both of us are in danger!

Holly stared at the angry young men, barely able to breathe. The spear points were very close and very sharp. Somewhere she found a scrap of courage.

"Listen to me," she said in the loudest voice she could muster. "I am the Maregi. In our time, your people and the red-haired people all live together. They have for hundreds of years. They aren't enemies anymore. It was an accident that Frederick came with me this time, but he won't hurt you!"

They muttered in disbelief and kept their weapons poised.

"Listen," Holly appealed, meeting each pair of eyes in turn. "This is a matter for Borekarek to decide. I am the Maregi, but even I don't understand my own power. Maybe Borekarek can explain what's happened here. Please, take us to see him."

Serak searched her face for a long moment. Then he stepped back. The others lowered their weapons. Serak caught Frederick's arm in a strong grip and pulled him forward. Holly saw him wince, but he didn't make a sound.

In a flash she recalled her fright the first time she'd come here, how she had panicked and run. *And I wasn't facing a bunch of guys with spears! Frederick must be completely terrified!* She could only imagine what he was feeling. She walked close beside him, trying to keep up with Serak's pace. "Don't worry," she whispered to him. "Borekarek is a good guy." Frederick made no sign that he'd heard her but stared straight ahead as if under a spell.

Borekarek's little hut was a hub of activity. The door-skin was pulled back, and warriors were ducking in and out. Evaken came out as Holly and the others drew near. Serak hailed him.

"An urgent matter for your master, Evaken," said Serak. "The Maregi has returned, but with her is one of the enemy. She says he is from her world. Borekarek must find the truth of the matter."

Holly saw Evaken's black eyes widen as he looked from Frederick to her and then back to Frederick. In an instant he disappeared inside, then quickly returned and drew them all into the hut.

The central fire was blazing, and several scarred and muscular warriors sat on skins in a circle around it. Each man wore a burnished leather cap on his head and had his weapons beside him. Holly glimpsed several women in the far corner, wrapping things in pieces of cloth or skin. One of them looked like Avartha. All eyes turned towards the intruders as Borekarek, once again wearing his bearskin, shuffled around the fire to the doorway. Frederick gasped at the sight of the leering bear head. Holly reached for his arm to reassure him, but Serak held him too tightly.

"Maregi!" said Borekarek. "You have returned! We did not understand why you were taken when you were!"

Holly pushed past Serak. "Borekarek, you've got to help me! Something really strange happened. This is my cousin from my world. He was holding the last pot just before it broke, and he came with me!"

Borekarek's eyes wandered over to Frederick. In the warm firelight the red hair blazed around Frederick's freckled face like a corona. He was frozen with fright and looked like he might pass out at any moment.

"Ah, yes," muttered Borekarek, a half-smile twitching at the side of his mouth. "The flame-coloured hair. Serak and his men were right to bring him to me. Yet he is not our enemy, I think." The old man reached out a clawed hand to touch Frederick's hair. Frederick recoiled in fear.

"Release him," commanded Borekarek, drawing back and nodding to Serak, who immediately let go of Frederick's arm. Frederick stood where he was, dazed, absently rubbing the arm and looking very small and lost. Holly felt a surge of pity. She'd spent almost every moment of the last two weeks staying as far away from Frederick as she could. But now . . . now everything was different. She laid a hand on his shoulder. "It's okay," she said to him. She was sure he heard her, but he made no answer.

"Serak," said Borekarek, "you must trust the Maregi when she tells you that this one is not an enemy but a friend."

"Very well, Borekarek," he said, his face still dark with suspicion. "But allow us to keep a watch on him just the same. You did but a few hours ago warn us of enemy spies."

"Yes, indeed, and you did well to seize him and bring him to me."

Serak bowed curtly, turned, and led his warriors away. As he left, Borekarek sighed and turned back to Frederick.

"Young man, do you understand the words we speak?" he asked.

Frederick nodded and tried to say something, but the word came out as a squeak.

"Good. You needn't be afraid of me," the sorcerer said, smiling. "I am Borekarek, the wizard of the Sun Circle. It is your cousin's great destiny to save us from our enemies."

Frederick's eyes widened, but he said nothing.

"Even you, young man, appear to have come here for a purpose. There is a pair of runes on the Salgren stick which I have puzzled over for many days. It appears with those runes which speak of the Maregi, but it seems to tell of another. The runes refer to the one who is and yet is not. This is obscure, and yet I doubt that Korak's magic would have allowed you to come here and understand our talk unless you were intended to do so."

Frederick's eyes flicked to Holly's face, then back to Borekarek's.

"You—you won't kill me, then?" Frederick croaked. Holly realized that these were the first words he'd spoken since they'd been captured by Serak's men. Clearly, he'd been expecting death at any moment, despite all her attempts to reassure him.

Borekarek shook his head. "No. But you must stand with us and not arouse any suspicions. As you have seen, Serak's men are hard to convince."

Frederick gulped and looked down at the dirt floor.

"Borekarek," growled one of the burly men by the fire, "we must continue with these plans."

"Ah, yes!" Borekarek shuffled over to them and sank down onto the skins.

Holly shot an uneasy glance at Frederick. He seemed to be breathing more freely now that the sorcerer had moved away.

"Frederick," she hissed, "Borekarek is the most powerful person here, and if he believes in you, the others have to."

"Where . . . where the bloody 'ell are we?"

"I know it's hard to believe, but we're at Stonehenge around 600 B.C., and the enemy invaders they're talking about are the Celts. There's some prophecy about me fighting the invaders. That's why they call me the Maregi."

"The Celts—like the Irish and the Welsh and whatnot?"

"Right. It was around this time that they first started coming here. That's why you have to be careful. They're suspicious of you."

"That's obvious, isn't it?"

She smiled at the familiar gruffness. "Just be careful."

"Is . . . is this what's been goin' on in the barn, then? You goin' back and forth in time?"

"Yes. You see why I couldn't tell you. You'd never have believed me. I didn't believe it myself at first."

"There must be some way, if we could only see it!" one of the warriors by the fire raised his voice in frustration.

Another man was shaking his head. "These machines give them the advantage over us."

Holly saw that a picture had been scratched into the hard dirt floor beside the fire pit. The men were bent over it, eyes squinting at the feathery lines.

"Let's take a look," she whispered to Frederick, pulling him nearer so they could both see the rough drawing.

The picture showed two wheels joined by a straight line, with two crudely drawn horses attached. It looked like a chariot. Holly recognized it from pictures in Dad's books about ancient Rome. Whoever had drawn this one had taken care to mark out the lines of the wheel spokes.

"That's a chariot, isn't it?" she asked.

The man nearest the drawing raised his head abruptly. "Do you have these machines in your world?"

"Not anymore. But people used to use them for fighting in wars."

Borekarek raised his eyes to hers. "Young Maregi, we need to understand these machines. They seem light as the wind—not like our own carts. The invaders use them to appear out of nowhere and descend upon us swiftly. If we could somehow damage these machines enough to delay the attack of our enemies until your power is at its full, we would have a chance against them. But if we do not delay the attack, it may be all over before you can help us."

Holly stared at the diagram. She thought of the pictures in Dad's books, but she had never studied them closely enough to see how the chariots were constructed. Why would she? But she suddenly had an idea.

"Frederick," she said, squeezing his arm. "You understand cars. Is a chariot wheel really so different from a car wheel?"

"A . . . a chariot wheel?" He gazed down at the diagram.

Holly watched his face a moment in the firelight. It was still there, that set of the jaw that always reminded her of the scowling toddler brandishing a plastic truck. But now there was something else she hadn't seen before. Maybe she had just never looked.

"Listen, Frederick, would it be hard to do something to chariot wheels that would make them need fixing before they could be used again? Like, maybe something that nobody would notice right away?"

"'Course not," Frederick shrugged. "Lots of things you could do. Cut the spokes, that would do it. Dead easy."

"Cut the spokes?" The first man shook his head. "Even from a distance, they look very sturdy. They are made of wood. It would take hours to cut through them."

Frederick frowned, then licked his lips. "Not if you had a drill."

"A drill?" asked Borekarek. "What is that?"

Frederick stood silent, face averted. Holly looked down at the holster on his belt. His hand twitched beside it.

"Frederick . . . show them," she said softly.

Reluctantly, Frederick pulled out the drill. He fished a drill bit out of his shirt pocket, fit it in and pulled the trigger. The machine whined. The warriors started and stared in wonder.

"Cordless, this one," Frederick said, fighting back a nervous smile. "Works on batteries."

"This is a great mystery," murmured one man. "We have not seen this magic before."

"It makes a noise," another pointed out.

"Yes, it does," agreed Borekarek. "But Evaken knows how to weave a spell of deafness that lasts a few minutes. Would that be enough time, young man?" he asked Frederick.

Frederick's head shot up as the implications sank in. "What? You mean me?"

"You're the only one who knows how to use a drill," Holly said.

"It's dead easy. Anyone could." Frederick stopped. The warriors were staring at him with a mixture of fear and wonder in their eyes.

"The invaders' camp is only a few miles from here," continued Borekarek. "You must find the chariots and disable them as quickly as possible. Evaken will go with you, since he is adept at a number of short-lived but useful spells. We have a hostage whose clothing you can wear to make you less conspicuous. Will you go?"

Frederick gaped at him, shaking his head. "I—I—" he stuttered.

"It will show our people that you are truly a friend and not an enemy," pointed out the man beside Borekarek.

"This may be what the runes have foretold," murmured the old sorcerer.

Frederick looked at Holly in dismay, then closed his mouth and squared his shoulders. "I've no choice, really, have I?"

"Not really," she told him uneasily.

Borekarek sighed in relief. "Evaken, fetch the hostage's garments for our young friend."

Within a few minutes Frederick had changed into the clothing of the captured enemy. He looked completely different, as if he had put on another skin, another life, along with the new clothes. Holly's stomach knotted as she watched Evaken strap a sheathed dagger around Frederick's waist beside the drill.

What have I done? He's in real danger now!

Everything was suddenly so complicated. Poor Frederick, being hustled off to the enemy camp against his will! As Evaken pushed him out the door, he turned once to glance helplessly at Holly, then disappeared into the gathering dusk.

She lingered at the doorway, chewing a fingernail as she watched the two figures melt into the trees at the bottom of the slope. *What if he gets killed out there?*

The knot in her stomach tightened as she realized she had no idea what was happening. Everything was out of control.

"Hhollee." A warm hand squeezed her shoulder. She turned to see Avartha's smiling face.

"Avartha!" Holly threw her arms around her. "Oh, Avartha! I was afraid I'd never see you again!"

Avartha hugged her tightly and smiled as they drew apart. "I was determined we should meet again, especially after you disappeared so quickly—"

"The fire!" Holly suddenly recalled in alarm. "Your house! Did it all get burned?"

Avartha nodded gravely. "Yes, there was little left. I saved Mother's loom and a few pots but nothing more. But we have all been staying at Sarum since then. I have a home for now."

"Oh, Avartha!" Holly squeezed her arm sympathetically,

noticing at the same moment that Avartha had pinned her brown cloak at one shoulder with the raven brooch.

Avartha followed her gaze and smiled again. "Yes, this too was saved." She picked up the bulging sack that had been sitting on the ground beside her. "Wait here a moment, Hhollee, while I take food to the young men, and then you must come in and share our evening meal."

Holly watched as Avartha walked among the young warriors milling about, handing out the wrapped packets that filled the sack. When she reached Serak, she lingered for a few moments, chatting easily. Then she turned, still smiling, and made her way back to Holly.

Holly followed her into the hut. Some of the warriors were gathering up their weapons, preparing to leave. Others had settled down with loaves of coarse bread and were still talking with Borekarek. Avartha led Holly to the back of the hut and handed her some bread and cheese. Holly was suddenly ravenous. Somewhere, back in that other life of hers, it was lunchtime.

"Eat," urged Avartha as they sat down in a dim corner together. "This may be our last meal until morning, depending—" she looked away suddenly.

"It's tonight, isn't it?" Holly asked around the chewy bread in her mouth. "The moon ceremony, or whatever it is."

Avartha nodded. "Yes. The ceremony and perhaps a battle—depending on your friend's success."

"Actually, he's my cousin, but I guess he's a friend too," she told Avartha, who stared at her in sudden surprise. Frederick, a friend? It was a new idea. "I guess you didn't hear me before when I told Borekarek. In my time, people have all different hair colours, even people in the same family."

Avartha shook her head, clearly alarmed. "I cannot imagine that. When Serak and I have children, I know what they will look like."

"Hold it. Serak and you?" It was Holly's turn to stare.

"He is my betrothed. Do you not do this in your world?"

"Well . . . not in my family. . . ."

"Our parents agreed to the betrothal when we were children. We have always known this. If the invaders are defeated, we will be married at the end of summer."

"But you're just a girl!"

"I will be fifteen summers old by then," said Avartha, a little proudly. "It is time I was married."

"Oh." Holly felt a sudden empty gulf yawn open between them.

Avartha smiled and squeezed Holly's hand. "Never mind, Maregi" she said. "Now we must think not of marriage but of this long, dark night. It belongs to you, and to all of us. You will sleep here until Borekarek calls us all to see the moon."

Holly sighed and looked away. "What time will that be?"

Avartha shook her head. "He says he does not know the time, only that it will be tonight. He will watch and wait and call us when the time comes. And then, Maregi, all eyes will be on you."

Holly's stomach knotted again. "That's what I'm afraid of. What if Borekarek is wrong? What if I have no power after all?"

Avartha took both Holly's hands in hers. "You do. I know that you do. Borekarek and Evaken told me of your wonderful . . . thing. The silver thing that makes a song."

"My flute," said Holly, pulling the case out of the back of her jeans. She opened it and fitted the flute together.

Avartha bent to caress the smooth silver. "It is a wondrous thing!"

Holly played a couple of scales, then a simple nursery rhyme tune. Avartha's eyes were wide.

"It—it is marvelous, Hhollee. I only hope that its power is great enough to save us when the time comes."

Holly's smile faded.

"Avartha," she said, "did Borekarek tell you that the enemies have your mother?"

Avartha looked away and blinked. "Yes," she said, her voice barely audible.

"I promise, if it's in my power, I'll get her back."

Suddenly, they heard shouts outside.

"Come!" Avartha pulled Holly to her feet.

They emerged into near-darkness. A slash of red still stained the western sky where the sun had set, but night had settled around the hill. Over in the east the full moon was rising, huge and solemn.

"They have returned!" someone called.

Holly followed Avartha from the hut and into a small crowd of young warriors gathered near the stone circle. She strained to peer over shoulders and heads, even though there was so little light that she could barely see. Someone lit a torch, and it flared up in the gloom. At that moment she caught sight of Frederick in his loose Celtic shirt and trousers labouring up the hillside, trying to keep up with Evaken.

When they reached the circle, Frederick looked about him awkwardly, brow streaming, breathing hard. Evaken stopped and grinned, then turned and grabbed Frederick's hand and held it high.

"Our enemies' chariots are crippled!" he shouted.

A surprised murmur rose from the crowd. Some shook their heads, while others crowded closer and a few cheered.

"It is true, friends!" Evaken continued. "We have been to

the enemy camp and have damaged their war machines! The spokes of every wheel are now filled with holes, and they will go no more than a few paces before they collapse! Be grateful to our friend here for bringing his wondrous machine from his world to ours!"

Evaken's voice didn't crack once throughout his little speech, and Holly smiled as she watched him clap the beaming Frederick on the shoulder. A murmur of approval rose around them. Relief flooded through her.

"You have given us this night, if not the dawn, young friend," roared Borekarek's voice in the dimness. "We owe you a great debt."

Cheers rose up then from the crowd. When they died down, Holly heard Serak's voice ringing out, ordering the warriors back to their posts. They all melted into the night, leaving Borekarek's hut quiet again.

Holly picked her way to Frederick's side. "Great work!" she said, suddenly shy and glad of the darkness that hid them from each other.

"That Evaken is fantastic!" he said, turning to her excitedly. "All the magic he knows—amazing! One of those Celtic blokes heard us muckin' about the chariots and come to have a look. I thought we were done for, but this Evaken just said a few words and this fellow walked away like he never heard a thing! And all he had to do to give me some light was cup his hand and say some other words!"

Holly listened to him in wonder. Was this really Frederick?

"Well, you certainly proved yourself tonight. I bet they'll trust you now."

Avartha came up with a cloak and wrapped it around Frederick's shoulders. Evaken took his arm and they all followed Borekarek into the hut.

Inside, Borekarek called for food and drink for the young heroes. Avartha brought bowls of cool water and milk and passed around the nutty bread and soft cheese that Holly had eaten earlier. *Not a kingly feast, but the glow of firelight on happy faces made it the best celebration she could remember.*

Avartha and Evaken were in high spirits, and Frederick smiled like she'd never seen him smile before. They oohed and ahhed over his watch with its luminous dial. When he demonstrated his drill on an old wooden bowl, they all laughed uproariously as a stream of water poured out of the hole. Borekarek's wrinkled old face was beaming, and even the bear head seemed to grin down at the happy company.

I want to bottle this moment, pour it into a pot and take it home with me, Holly thought wistfully.

All too soon, Borekarek lurched to his feet.

"You must rest now, all of you," he said. "There is no sleep for me this night, for I must watch the moon. You especially must sleep now, Maregi," he said to Holly. "This time, I know you will not leave us."

The fire was burning low, and Avartha led Holly back to the pile of skins in the corner, where Holly had left her flute earlier.

"Sleep well, Hhollee," said Avartha with a smile and left her.

Holly sank down on the soft bed and curled up, cradling the flute in one arm. Across the room, Evaken and Frederick settled in a corner near the door. Avartha lay down in the shadows nearby. In a few moments the sounds of measured breathing merged with the soft hissing of the embers in the fire pit.

Holly could not sleep. *It's only noon at home,* she told herself. But it was more than that. A potent mixture of excitement and fear kept her on edge. And she was filled with longing too, a longing to stay here with these people and yet at the same time to go home. When she closed her eyes she saw Dad's face, and Mum's. Mum.

She sat up. The hut was very dark now that the fire was almost out. A sliver of moonlight showed beneath the door-skin. Holly crawled towards it on her hands and knees. As she reached the doorway, she thought she heard someone stir. But she kept going until she had slipped outside.

Borekarek sat on a low stool by the door, leaning against the wall of the hut. The moon was high now. Beyond the huddled shadows of the hut, Stonehenge blazed white on its hilltop.

"Borekarek!" Holly whispered, standing up.

The old man grunted. His shadow moved slightly.

"Maregi?"

"Yes. I can't sleep. Can I ask you something?"

"Certainly, young one."

Holly crouched down beside him and gazed up at the two shadowy faces, one human, one animal.

"Borekarek, could there be more than one Maregi?"

"No, my child. Why do you ask?"

"Because . . . because I found out some weird things last time I was back in my own time. My mother—this was before I was born—she . . . I think she heard the music from the pots too."

Borekarek coughed. "You must be mistaken."

"Maybe. But I found out she used to play music too, and that suddenly one day she got really scared, dropped her instrument in the barn, and never played again. And where she had been playing that day . . . it was just outside the room with the pots."

"Mmm," said Borekarek. "Curious."

"Yeah. The thing is, I never knew she played. She's been really . . . angry at me for spending so much time at it. Until Aunt Sally—that's Frederick's mum—told me about it, I had no idea Mum was into music when she was young. It was like this huge secret."

"Mmm," Borekarek said again.

"And the clincher is, when *I really, really didn't want to come back here,* and I tried to practise far away from the pot room, the music of the pots came to me anyway. I just couldn't get away from it. And I think maybe that's what happened to Mum too."

Borekarek was silent for a long time. Then he shifted and looked down at her.

"Maregi, Korak's power is a mystery, as much a mystery as life itself. I do not understand it fully. But this much I do know: fate and choice are bound together in an endless dance. Your mother may have heard a Call, although it was not I who did the Calling. But she refused the Call. You, my child, did not. You may not think so, but you chose to come here. And so you are the Maregi."

Holly gazed out at the plain awash in moonlight and knew it was true.

"Yes," she said softly. Then she stood up. "Thanks, Borekarek."

And she crawled back into the blackness of the hut, found her flute and curled up again.

IT WAS VERY COLD when she was shaken awake. She started up from a deep slumber, dimly aware of a light near her eyes.

"Hhollee! Wake up!" came an urgent whisper.

She sat up quickly, trying to focus on the flame of the rush-light and the face behind it.

"Evaken has run to Sarum to bring the people. The moon-darkness has begun."

Avartha handed her a small bowl of milk. "They will be some time in arriving, but we have preparations to complete while we wait."

Holly sat and sipped the milk while Avartha stirred the fire back to life. She looked across the room and saw Frederick sitting up. He glanced awkwardly at her across the fire-pit.

Holly groped about in the shadows for the jacket she had left here the time before. There it was, stuffed down between the skins and the wall. She struggled into it, then tucked the flute into one of the inside pockets and zipped the jacket up. She might as well be warm. Then she followed Avartha outside into the chill night air.

She looked up. The full moon was on its way down its western arc. It looked like someone had taken a bite out of it.

"Come," said Avartha, taking her arm and steering her towards the circle. The moonlight was still bright, and she was able to walk fairly easily. But something else was different. There was tension in the air; she could feel it. She could hear soft rustlings in the night: the vague *hush, hush* of quiet feet, the hiss of in-drawn breaths, the dull clink of metal.

Borekarek was standing in the middle of the stone circle, hands clasped together, looking up at the moon.

"Um . . . what am I supposed to do, Borekarek?" she asked in a whisper, lingering outside the circle.

He looked at her and smiled. "Nothing just now. Evaken has run to Sarum, and Serak's men are making ready below. One scout has sighted our enemies, but they are still far off. Yet you should know the important parts of the Circle, which I believe will be the focus of your power. Come."

He held out his hand, and she stepped through the outer

ring of stones and on into the inner horseshoe comprised of five sets of two pillars with their crosspieces, the things that Dad's book called trilithons. Borekarek pointed out the centre of the horseshoe, then indicated the trilithon that had framed the setting sun. Almost above it now was the sinking moon, slowly being swallowed by blackness.

"We must watch it carefully."

"But what do I watch for?"

"For the night to eat the moon. I believe your power will surge when the moon is completely swallowed, but you must trust your heart, Maregi. Watch, and wait . . . and act when you feel you must."

Holly looked at Borekarek in alarm. But at the same time she knew what he meant. She was the Maregi. Only she would know what to do. She followed him back out of the circle in silence.

With a start she saw that Evaken had returned and was standing near the door of the hut, talking to Frederick. Frederick had discarded the Celtic outfit and was now dressed in the leather tunic and tight leggings of Borekarek's people rather than the loose Celtic trousers. He was belting a sheathed dagger around his waist.

"Frederick!" she cried as she understood. "What do you think you're doing? You're not going to fight, are you?"

"Suppose I might be of some use," he mumbled.

"But you might get hurt! You might get killed!"

"And what about you, then?" he said defiantly. "We're both in the same mess, aren't we?"

"I—well, I have some sort of power, I hope. . . ." she said lamely. The knot in her stomach wound tighter than ever. And there was something else, an uneasy feeling that she'd missed something important about Frederick's presence here.

"Our people are coming," said Borekarek.

She saw them then. They advanced in a cloud of legs and bobbing leather helmets, women and men and children together, weapons glinting in the dwindling moonlight. Holly saw the grim, determined faces as the first of them drew near. Her heart sank as she realized how few of them there were. She shivered but turned back to Frederick.

"Good luck," she said. He nodded once and left.

"Hhollee, this is for you," said Avartha behind her. Holly stared at the cloaklike thing that Avartha held out to her. She reached out a hand and touched it. It was made of feathers. Black feathers.

"This belonged to Korak, our famous seer," she said. "It has been carefully kept by every sorcerer after him, waiting for the time when Maregi would one day wear it. Here."

Holly slipped it on over her jacket. There were small arm-holes, and when she slid her arms through them, she had wings.

"Try to become a war-goddess for a while, if you can," said Borekarek with a grim smile.

"The moon!" someone shouted.

The moon was more than half gone now. A chill darted up Holly's spine.

Breathlessly, she fumbled in her jacket pocket. She drew out the flute and willed her trembling fingers to obey her. Softly she breathed into it, testing its sound.

She glanced again at the moon. The white sliver was even smaller now. Her heart was racing. If Borekarek had read his runes wrong, she might be powerless. If the Celts were stealing through the dark towards them, they could overwhelm these people, determined as they were. She and Frederick could both be killed. She would never see Mum and Dad again, together or apart. That thought almost choked her.

Suddenly, Borekarek was beside her. "Come, Maregi. It is time."

She followed him back inside the circle. This time the tingle of power that had gripped her that first day was back, crackling all around her. Borekarek stood before her, facing the west, arms flung to the sky. The last sliver of moon touched the top of the trilithon.

Borekarek's mighty voice rose up, clear on the still night air, uttering strange words that Holly could not understand. The crowd beyond the circle shouted back a response.

This is it! This is my moment!

Holly raised the flute to her lips. She drew a deep breath and blew.

CHAPTER ELEVEN
WHEN NIGHT EATS THE MOON

HOLLY HAD NO IDEA WHAT SHE WOULD PLAY before the first note sounded, but suddenly music filled her to the brim and her fingers moved on their own. Sound leaped out of her flute as the last whisper of moonlight flared along its silver sides.

As the music surrounded her, it seemed to detach itself from her lips and breath and fingers and become something other. It bounced off the massive stones around her, eddied and flipped and echoed down from the burning stars above. She stood locked in a cocoon of sound. Then, as a rising wind moaned among the stones, she saw the light.

It looked like a seamless sheet of luminous green. It streamed from her feet and stretched away from her to the moon's horizon, vast and flat and paper-thin. Above it, the blackness swallowing the moon paused and left one curved blade of light in the western sky. All around it, the fierce stars shivered and halted in their courses. Time seemed to stop and hold its breath.

"Do you know what you see, Maregi?" said a craggy voice. Holly lowered her flute in astonishment and searched for the speaker. The music continued without her as her eyes found the shadowy figure of an old man, balanced on the inner edge of the light.

"No."

"This is the garment of time. You have the power, Maregi, to rend this cloth and weave it anew, to change it forever. But such a thing must not be done lightly."

She stared at him, then at the light. "I don't understand."

"Look closely," said the old man, suddenly beside her. At once she saw differently, as if through a magnifying glass. The sheet of light was not seamless after all, but was composed of countless tiny strands woven together in an intricate interlace. Where one strand ended, others were woven in to take its place.

"See here," he said, pointing. "These threads are Borekarek's people. They are not strong enough to resist the invaders. The question is, will they be slaughtered, and their pattern abruptly rent from the fabric? Or will they be woven into the larger pattern?"

Holly looked. "So, you mean this is history, and I can change it?"

He nodded. "Yes."

"So . . . I could let the Celts be defeated, and save Borekarek's people."

"You could. But consider well: How would this affect your world?"

Holly shivered suddenly. Would all the people whose Celtic ancestors came from Britain be wiped out? And what would happen to Frederick, to Mum, and Dad? What would happen to her? If she allowed their ancestry to be changed, who would they be?

"This is too much power," she whispered.

"It is," the shadow nodded. "But you have the power to

weave as well as to rend. The pattern is for you to decide, Maregi."

He smiled. And then he was gone.

The pattern is for you to decide.

Holly stood frozen, robed in music and eddying light. Far off on the plain, through the luminous sheet, she thought she glimpsed the shadows of a gathering army, the glint of pale moonlight on swords. She heard the harsh braying of trumpets on the wind. They were coming, and coming swiftly. And there were so many of them, so many more than the group she had seen around the fire. Too many of them for these determined few crowded around the towering stones. There would be slaughter.

Unless I choose to stop the Celts.

Her flute weighed heavily in her hand. A memory floated back to her:

Dad's face, beaming and proud.

"Piper, some day you'll get so good at that you'll lead the whole world off and away into some beautiful country we've never dreamed of."

Was that her task? No. Not to escape destiny, but to weave together its frayed edges.

But how?

It seemed that she stood there forever in an agony of uncertainty, wrapped in light and song. Through the glow she could see the upturned faces of Borekarek's people, a people with hope in their eyes. And beyond them the invaders advanced, coming nearer every moment. Beside her stood Borekarek, dazzled by the light surrounding her. And behind him, just outside the circle of Stonehenge, she glimpsed Frederick.

Frederick.

She tucked her flute into her jacket and turned resolutely to Borekarek.

"Borekarek," she said, "Your enemies are coming. They've left their chariots behind, but there are so many of them that you don't stand a chance."

Borekarek looked at her, dazed and puzzled. "Maregi . . . this powerful light . . . Can it not turn them back?"

Holly shook her head, choking on the word. "No."

"Maregi, you are our one hope. Has your power been revealed to you?"

"Yes." She felt like she'd swallowed a stone. "I think Korak spoke to me. He told me what I have to do."

She took the old man's wrinkled hands in hers and squeezed them tight. "Borekarek, I'm sorry, but the thing I have to do . . . you're not going to like it."

Borekarek stared at her in dismay.

"Remember you once told me, 'There are many ways of fighting and of winning'? Well, the only way you and your people can win is if you agree to make peace with your enemies and share the land. Otherwise, you'll all die. There's an ocean of them out there. They'll wipe you out."

"But—but the prophecy . . . You are the Maregi! The Maregi was supposed to save us—"

"I *am* saving you. Just not the way you thought. You said yourself you weren't sure what the Maregi was supposed to do. But now *I'm* sure." Through welling tears she gazed up at his ancient face, lit now by the pulsing light around her. "I'm so sorry, Borekarek. But this is why I came."

She squeezed his hands once more, then forced herself to let go and turn away. Once more she gazed out across the plain. The Celts were very close now, but they had halted a short distance from Stonehenge and were shielding their eyes from the light. It gleamed on a forest of polished metal helmets, long shields and swords. This moment might not come again.

"Wait here, Borekarek," she said, then walked between the stone pillars and down the slope to the Heel Stone.

Behind her, Holly heard the shouts of the warriors who had caught sight of their enemies. There was the dreadful hiss of weapons being drawn from wooden and leather sheaths. She clenched her fists. She could almost taste the fear and the lust for blood on both sides. She stood poised between two seething armies.

It's now or never.

She reached into her pocket for the flute, realizing as she did so that she still wore the black feathered cloak.

I can use it now.

Quickly she stepped out in front of the Heel Stone and played a wild arpeggio on her flute. The notes rang out across the plain and mingled with the earlier song that still echoed among the stones, and the veil of light that clung to her burned more brightly. Swiftly, she raised her arms to the sky. The feathered cloak billowed out from her sides as her arms became wings and she became a black bird-shadow. The greenish light glowed on her shimmering wings.

"Halt!" she bellowed at the Celts. "I am the Maregi, the protector of these people! Who are you who dare to approach this sacred place and claim this land by force? I am the Raven! Why do you attack my people?"

Am I crazy? They'll never fall for it!

But she heard the hiss of in-drawn breaths like a wave on the sea.

What was that name? The name of the war-goddess? Cathu . . . something?

"I am Cathubodua! Hear me!" she shouted.

I guessed right!

She saw the first ranks shrink back in fear. She saw the older man Ankios kneel where he was, dropping his sword in front of him.

Heart pounding, Holly plunged down the slope and into the crowd of cowering Celts. They shuddered and cried out as she came among them; many ran. But Holly ignored them and waded through the forest of bodies and shields and spears until she found the man she wanted: Camanom. She gripped him by the shoulder and pulled him to his feet.

"Come with me," she commanded.

She dragged him back with her and pulled him right inside the stone circle.

"Borekarek!" she called, reaching for the edge of his bear-cloak and tugging him towards her.

She drew the two men together until they stood face to face, wrapped with her in a cloak of light and song, with the garment of time shimmering around them.

"You have to make peace, not war," she told them. "Your two peoples have to become one. You have to share this land, not fight over it."

The two men stood speechless.

Then Borekarek growled, "They have killed our people and burned our storehouses!"

"They have slain some of our best warriors and taken others hostage!" said Camanom.

"That is all in the past," said Holly firmly, "and the killing has to stop. And it *will* stop right now, right here. I am the Maregi, and I command it!"

They both stared at her, caught between doubt and awe.

Swiftly she turned and walked again from the stone circle

to find Frederick in the shadows nearby. He looked as dazed as the others, but she tugged at his sleeve.

"Frederick!" she hissed at him. "Please come! I need you!" She pulled him back inside the circle with her, and to her surprise he didn't resist.

She drew him into the light with Borekarek and Camanom.

"This is my cousin," she said to them. "Look at us both, and see us as a sign from the future that your two peoples can become one and live in peace together. And it can happen without any more deaths. If you choose to make it happen."

Camanom stared at Frederick, open-mouthed.

Holly turned to him and shook him. "Camanom, I've chosen you because you are the only one who speaks the language of both races. You have to be the go-between, the peacemaker. Do you understand?"

He gaped at her for a moment, then nodded.

"Yes," he said slowly. "I understand."

"Then go! Win your people over! Tell them that the raven is the goddess not only of battle, but also of peace and protection!"

She gave him a little push, and he staggered out of the light, out of the circle, and ran down the hillside to his people.

"Borekarek, do you understand?" she asked, turning back to him, heartsick at the despair etched on his face.

"Yes," he said heavily. "Your power is clear. If this is what Korak intended, who am I to resist fate?"

The light and music were fading around her. Quickly, taking Frederick's arm on one side and Borekarek's on the other, she pulled them both with her to face Serak and his gathered army.

"Listen to me!" she cried. "You must make peace with these people, not war! They're ready to come to terms with you, to share the land with you. You have to be like Frederick and me—part of the same family, not enemies! This is the word of the Maregi!"

A gasp of shock rose around her.

"How can this be?" the people murmured.

Borekarek stepped forward and raised his arms. "Listen!" he roared. "The Maregi was sent to save us from death! If this is the only way, then we must choose to live!"

As he spoke, a voice called out from the huddled crowd. "Look! The sun!"

They all turned. There on the eastern horizon, beyond the Heel Stone, a pale light was seeping into the world. Holly whirled about and looked west; the moon had emerged from the eclipse and was already fading in the lightening sky. What had happened to the night?

"Evaken!" called Borekarek, hurrying back to the centre of the circle. Evaken was instantly at his side. The streak of light in the eastern sky was growing, and they both faced it.

"They will not take from us this celebration of the glory of our greatest god!" Borekarek roared.

The Heel Stone, framed by one of the huge stone gates, jabbed at the brightening streak in the sky. Then suddenly, in an explosion of red and gold, the burning edge of the sun burst along the side of the Heel Stone.

A great shout rose from the gathered crowd. As the ball of the sun slid up the left side of the stone, Borekarek's voice boomed out, strong and deep and ageless as Holly had never heard it before. He sang a strange song, and voices all around the circle replied. It sounded like a song of celebration, a celebration of light and of hope.

Hope? Holly thought bitterly. *Yes, but not the kind of hope they'd hoped for.*

"Let us talk!"

Holly turned to see a small delegation of Celtic warriors slowly approaching, led by Camanom. Their song finished, Borekarek's people fell silent. Many of their faces were dark with anger. Borekarek walked out between two of the pillar-stones and stopped in front of the Celts.

"We seek terms for peace," said Camanom in Borekarek's language.

"The terms must be equal," growled Borekarek.

"They shall be," replied Camanom with a slight bow. "First, as a token of our good will, we return to you the captive woman." Avartha and Evaken's mother, Vedda, walked forward through the press of warriors and sought the faces of her children.

"Mama!" Avartha's cry pierced the uneasy muttering of both sides as she ran forward from the shadows and embraced her.

"In return," continued Camanom, "We ask that you show us your desire for peace by giving one of your women in marriage to a nobleman of our people."

Dark heads hesitated, then nodded uncertainly and mumbled assent.

"It is agreed," said Borekarek.

"Good," said Camanom, stepping forward and laying a hand on Avartha's arm as she wept and embraced her mother. "I claim this woman for my wife. May our marriage be a sign of a new beginning for our two peoples."

Silence fell. Avartha slowly raised a tear-stained face as the meaning of the words caught her.

"Me?" she gasped in horror. "No! No, I am betrothed!"

Camanom's face was set. The hands of the Celts behind him twitched towards the weapons at their belts.

"No!" screamed Holly.

What have I done?

She leaped towards Avartha. But her body was suddenly paralyzed with dread as her ears began to buzz. Her last scream floated away from her, disembodied. She could only watch helplessly as Serak ran forward, his anguished face lit by the rising sun.

CHAPTER TWELVE
CALLS

THE COLD FLAGSTONES HIT HOLLY LIKE THE punch of a fist. The last pot lay in pieces around her.

I can never go back! Never!

Holly sobbed uncontrollably. She cried for Avartha, for Borekarek, for Serak and all the other people whose lives would never be the same. She cried for herself, for the fate that had forced her to betray the people she'd come to love.

Slowly, she became aware of a pain in her left shoulder. She sat up. The flute was still in her jacket pocket, poking into her. She sniffed and felt for it, realizing at the same time that she still wore the black feather-cloak. The memories flooded back and sobs shook her again. In a rage she tore off the cloak and flung it on the floor beside her.

A lot of good it did them after saving it for hundreds of years!

She rifled through her jacket pockets until she found a well-worn tissue to blow her nose.

Then suddenly she noticed Frederick. He was sitting in the doorway with his back against the ancient door jamb, knees drawn up to his chest. He eyed her miserably.

"Sorry," she mumbled, red-faced, mortified at her flood of tears.

"Here," he said, reaching over to stuff a large cloth handkerchief into her hand. "It's clean. Good job I pulled it out of my jeans."

Holly blew her nose, then looked at him again as his meaning sank in. He was still wearing the leather tunic and leggings.

"Your drill," she sniffed. "Did you leave it there too?"

"Nah. Dad's best drill, this is. Wouldn't let it out of my sight for anything." He patted the leather holster at his waist, and she saw that he had strapped the whole belt on close to the sheath of the dagger.

"Can we go back, then? Clear things up?" he asked hopefully.

"No, no," Holly shook her head. "That was the last pot. We can never go back. I'll never know what happened to everybody—whether Avartha really had to marry that guy Camanom, or anything! That's what's so awful!"

"Why'd we come back so sudden like that?"

Holly sniffed again. "Each pot had only a little piece of time in it, put in there long ago by a famous seer named Korak. When the amount of time in each pot ran out, that was it. There was no way to stay any longer. You just came back."

"What . . . what happened, then? When you were in that circle with all the light and what-not, and then you grabbed that other bloke and me. What was all that about?"

Holly drew a ragged breath. "I had the power to change history, to make the Celts go away even though history says that they settled here."

"Cor!"

"Yeah, sounds great, doesn't it? But I realized I couldn't do it. It would change everything in this world now, including

144

probably our whole family. So I had no choice. I had to make them go for peace instead of wiping each other out. That's why you were important; they had to see that someone with red hair didn't necessarily have to fight with the dark-haired people."

"Pretty amazing, that is!"

"Yeah," Holly said bitterly, "except look what it led to. A trap! I got trapped into doing the worst thing for the people who trusted me. And my friend Avartha has to marry some stranger she's never even seen before, probably somebody who has killed some of her own people. It's awful."

Frederick was silent for a long time. "Well, seems to me, if you had no choice, you can't blame yourself."

"Can't I? I don't know." She drew her knees up and put her head down on her arms, hiding her face from him.

Frederick cleared his throat. "I'm sorry. I really am. And I'm sorry I shouted and said all that rubbish before."

Holly raised her head, struggling to recall. A few fragments of their argument came floating back.

"I'm really sorry I wrecked your vacation in Portugal. I didn't know."

Frederick snorted. "Portugal! This was loads better than Portugal. It's the best time I ever had."

She stared at him. "Really?"

"Really."

"But how can you say that? You almost got killed back there!"

"I suppose," he said, staring down at his hands for a moment. "But I didn't, did I? And it was . . . exciting. A real adventure. Ever so much better than boring old England."

Holly gazed across the dim room. Frederick's face was silhouetted in the doorway.

"There's something else," he said, shifting uncomfortably. "I—what I mean is, I heard some of what you said . . . last night, or whenever it was. To the wizard. About your mum. Sorry—I couldn't help hearing, with no door and all. . . ."

Holly drew a deep breath. A strange gladness warmed her, surprised her. "It's okay. I'm glad you heard. I'm sick of keeping all these secrets. I'm *drowning* in secrets!"

"D'you think she went back there too, then? Your mum?"

Holly shook her head. "No. I don't think she broke any pots. She just heard the music and freaked out. She ran. Ran all the way to Vancouver."

"What I don't understand is, if you're the Maggie-what's-it, what was she? It makes no sense."

Holly shook her head. "I don't really understand that part either. Borekarek said that she was called but refused the call. Something about fate and choice bound together. I don't know."

Frederick coughed. "Well, it does explain a few things, doesn't it? Explains a lot, really. Her not wanting to come back here all those years. I overheard Granny and Granddad talking once or twice, but they were very tight-lipped about it."

Holly sighed. "I kept thinking there at the end that it could have been her and not me. But I'm glad it *was* me, after all. It's funny: I was only back there four times, but it started to feel almost like home."

Frederick glanced at her cautiously. "Tell me—that is, if you want to—tell me about the other times."

Holly told him. She told him about finding the pots and about meeting Borekarek and Avartha for the first time. She pulled out the raven amulet to show him. She told him about the bleeding head and the raiders setting fire to Avartha's house and carrying off her mother. She recited as much of the weird prophecy as she could remember and described the encounter with the Celts in the woods and her mad dash across the plains at night. She told him about the shape-changing raven on the library steps and about Aunt Sally's questions at the café.

"She asked me if I'd seen a ghost," she said, shaking her head. "I said no. I just couldn't tell her what was really going on!"

"A ghost!" Frederick snorted. "She would say that. Grand-dad was sure he'd seen a little ghost dog trotting round the barn here. Belonged to some ancestor, he said. Called it a cheerful little spirit. She probably thought you'd seen something like that."

Holly sighed. "So maybe a ghost would've been easier to talk about. But who'd believe all this stuff about time travel? Do you think she would?"

Frederick shook his head. "I've no idea if she'd believe that. . . . Hang on! What's the time?" he said, suddenly sitting up straighter and peering at his watch. "Cor! It's a quarter past twelve!" He struggled to his feet. "She'll be back by now!"

Holly gazed up at him in horror. "You're right! We'd better get out of here!"

He offered her a hand and pulled her up. "This gear of mine'll take some explaining. . . ." Frederick looked down and tugged at the leather tunic that fell past his waist over the leggings. "And I've left my bloody jeans back at Stonehenge!"

Holly chewed her lip. "If she's already back, we've got to get you into the house without her noticing."

Frederick started down the corridor, then suddenly stopped and gazed back into the room. "We'd better close this up then, hadn't we?"

"I guess." Holly was suddenly overwhelmed with sadness

again. The feather cloak was a desolate pool of blackness on the floor. She stepped back inside and buried her fingers in it. It was weightless, like a cloud. Part of her wanted to keep this marvelous thing. But no. It seemed to belong here in Korak's secret room. She gazed wistfully at the empty shelf and at the broken shards of pottery that littered the floor. On impulse she scooped up two of the larger pieces. She held out one of them to Frederick.

"Here. A souvenir."

"Thanks." He flashed her another rare smile. Then with a sigh she pulled the old door shut.

Thud. A hollow sound.

Halfway down the passage, she stopped and turned. She pulled her flute out of her jacket pocket and played one long, solemn note. Then she listened. Nothing. Nothing at all but silence.

"The magic is gone," she said. Frederick nodded.

Then they both hurried out to the barn door.

They paused in the shadow of the half-open door and peered out. Aunt Sally's red car was parked in the shade of the big oak tree.

"Bloody 'ell," said Frederick, scowling.

Holly thought fast. "Do you have anything in the garage? Some overalls or something? Something you could put on over this stuff just until you get inside to change?"

"Brilliant!" he said with a sudden, radiant grin. "If I could just hop across to the garage without her seeing. . . ."

"How about I go into the house first, start talking to her, distract her. . . ."

"Right, that's good, that. Mustn't come in together—she'd be really suspicious then." He smiled at her ruefully.

Holly grinned back at him. "You're right. Okay. Wait till I

148

get inside and get her talking. Then you can run into the garage."

"Right."

She slipped outside and walked across the sunny yard. Birds were singing, and a light breeze stirred the leaves of the oak tree. A perfect, peaceful summer day.

"Hi, Aunt Sally," she called in her cheeriest voice as she strolled down the back hallway and into the kitchen.

"'Allo!" said Aunt Sally, not looking up as she pulled a meat pie from the oven. "I was about to call you. . . ." She stopped, staring. "What on earth have you been up to? And why the heavy-weather gear?"

Holly's heart sank as she looked down at her clothes. Her shirt was stained with mud, and so were her running shoes. Her dirty jeans now had a hole in one knee. And then there was her rain jacket with its bulging pockets.

"Um . . . it seemed really cool when I went out earlier," she muttered lamely.

"And that's a nasty scratch, that is!" Aunt Sally pointed to Holly's cheek. "What have you been doing, then?"

Holly's mind raced. She'd been too busy worrying about Frederick to think of herself. What could she say? Where else had she been where it was wet or muddy or prickly—other than Avartha's world? Emily's pasture? No. The backyard? No. The overgrown fields up the hill? Yes! She saw again Mum's swing, swaying there alone in the sunshine. She'd had to wade through long, tangled grass to get there, and she vaguely recalled seeing a dead branch or two on the ground beside the tree. And a person could easily fall off an old swing, right?

"Well, um . . ." She shifted from one foot to the other. "I went for a walk through the pasture and up the hill to the tree at the top. And I found a swing—Mum's old swing, I guess.

The one in the picture you have." The story was knitting itself together as she spoke. "And I sat on it and swung for a while, but it sort of—well, I guess the ropes are kind of old and I lost my balance and fell off. . . . And I fell onto some prickly dead branches on the ground . . . and then I slipped on a muddy patch trying to get up." Holly stopped herself.

Enough! She'll never buy that!

She held her breath as Aunt Sally frowned.

"You ought to know better than to get on an old thing like that, love," she said. "It hasn't been used for years and years. Granny and Granddad never let Frederick swing on that one. I doubt anyone has been up that hill since Granddad died. I know I haven't. The grass must be all a-tangle."

Fantastic! So she didn't know whether it's muddy or not!

"I'm sorry," Holly hung her head. "I wasn't thinking. I just saw the swing, and it looked so inviting."

"Well, never mind," said Aunt Sally, bustling away and hauling some plates out of the cupboard.

"We'll have a look at that scratch of yours later. This steak and kidney pie's getting cold. You go and wash up then, love, and I'll see if I can find Frederick."

Frederick had just eased himself through the back door and was tiptoeing down the hall to his room. Aunt Sally caught sight of him. Holly saw in relief that his grey overalls covered the leather tunic and leggings perfectly.

"There you are, Frederick!" said Aunt Sally. "Be quick, now. Your dinner's getting cold."

"Right, Mum," he mumbled, hurrying off down the hall.

Holly slipped out of her muddy shoes and ran to her room. She ripped off the jacket and T-shirt, and pawed through her jumble of clothes for another pair of jeans. As she tucked her clean shirt in, she glanced in the mirror. That scratch on her cheek was pretty red. Would that silly story satisfy Aunt Sally's curiosity?

She almost bumped into Frederick as she burst out of her room. Their eyes met briefly. She smiled; he smiled back. And she knew in that moment that they had silently agreed on something terribly important: Aunt Sally must know nothing about their adventure together.

We can't let her suspect a thing!

Holly hung back as Frederick turned and loped into the kitchen ahead of her. She followed more slowly, pretending to ignore him.

But as Holly sat and watched Aunt Sally dishing out the pie, everything seemed normal. In fact, blissfully normal. Frederick ate hunched over and silent as usual. Aunt Sally chattered on about her friends on the town council and the new museum that was opening thanks to the efforts of the historical society. Holly was barely listening. The rich, meaty smell of the pie wafted up from her plate, and she realized with a shock how intensely glad she was to be back in her own world. Here was Aunt Sally's bright kitchen with its smug, cheerful plants and the blue place-mats that looked like scraps of summer sky. Everything seemed to shine with a sudden clarity—the polished pine table, her own pale hands holding knife and fork, the wisp of steam rising from the teapot. In a flash she recalled her panic back there in the fading moonlight, when she'd realized she might never see Mum or Dad again.

Now I will! I'm safe now!

"What about you then, Frederick?" she heard Aunt Sally asking. "What've you been up to this morning?"

Holly glanced over at him anxiously. She could see his right knee pumping up and down just beneath the table.

"Patched the floor of the Morris," he said, jabbing his fork at the remaining mound of meat pie. He didn't look up.

"Mmm, good. What did you use for a patch?"

"Found some old scrap metal in the barn. Granddad left some in there. Showed me once."

"Oh, good," she said. "Sounds a good deal safer than Holly's little adventure."

Frederick's head shot up, and he looked at Holly in barely concealed alarm.

She felt her face flush, but took a quick breath, slapped a sheepish smile on her face and said, "I was telling your mum about falling out of that old swing at the top of the hill. It's stupid, I know. I should never have gone and sat on it." She saw relief wash over his face before he turned quickly back to his plate.

"The ropes broke, then?" asked Aunt Sally.

"No . . . just frayed." Holly stared into her mug of tea. *Now I'm in big trouble if she goes and checks!*

"Well, I expect I'll not have to worry about you doing that again," said Aunt Sally. "I'll have a look at that scratch in a minute. I've some good salve we can put on it."

Holly mopped up the last of her gravy with a piece of pie crust. Silence settled over them. Holly nervously smoothed out the fringe of her place-mat; Frederick scraped at a tiny chip on his mug with one fingernail. The only sounds were the sipping of hot tea and the ticking of the kitchen clock on the wall.

Suddenly, Aunt Sally got up and whisked the empty plates off the table. She turned the taps on and reached for the bottle of washing up liquid.

Frederick shot a hopeful glance at Holly and pushed his chair back. "Awright if I . . . get on with the old Morris then, Mum?"

"Yes, off you go." Aunt Sally didn't even look at him.

He glanced once more at Holly. There was a gleam of triumph in his eyes. Then he shuffled towards the back door and disappeared outside.

Holly lingered uneasily. *I should offer to do the dishes,* she thought. *But if I do that, she'll maybe want to talk.*

She clenched her fists and forced the words out. "Can I help, Aunt Sally?"

"No, no, love—there's just these few things. Oh, I almost forgot!" She turned suddenly, hands covered in suds. "That scratch of yours! Come on, then." Aunt Sally dried her hands quickly and hustled Holly down the hall to the bathroom.

Holly stood watching herself in the mirror as Aunt Sally drew a tube of some sort of clear ointment from the medicine cabinet. She dabbed a bit of it along the scratch.

Holly winced. She stared at the long red line, still so bright, as if those branches had whipped her face only this morning. . . . Well, come to think of it, it *was* only this morning, wasn't it? Two nights and a day ago in Avartha's world, but only a few hours ago here. She started at the memory.

"Does that sting, love?"

"A bit."

"Well, this will help it heal up right quick. There, then. Try not to touch it." Aunt Sally stepped back to survey her handiwork in the mirror, and Holly realized in a moment of panic that the amulet had flipped out of her shirt collar.

But Aunt Sally didn't seem to notice. She was already screwing the cap back on the ointment tube.

"Um . . ." said Holly nervously, "Would it be okay if I had a bath? I—"

"Why not, love? It'll ease your sore muscles. Always a bit of a shock when you have a fall like that. Just mind you don't wash all this salve off." And she bustled out before Holly could say another word.

She felt suddenly light-headed, and grabbed the bathroom sink for support. Sunshine streamed through the window just as it had when she'd first gone outside that morning. She was dizzy with all that had happened, with juggling all these worries at once, worries about Avartha, about Mum, and now Aunt Sally. Well, maybe she didn't have to worry so much about Aunt Sally. If she could just remember to be careful. . . .

She sank gratefully into the hot water and lay there with her head half submerged, waiting for the heat to nudge some of the kinks out of her body. Steam eddied around the room as she added more and more hot water. She wanted to stay here forever, with the weight of the amulet pressing against her skin. She gripped the smooth raven figure tightly and closed her eyes as Avartha's face swam into focus again.

Avartha! I ruined everything! And I never even got to say good-bye!

HOLLY LAY ON HER BED, exhausted, fingering the crumpled paper with the resort phone number on it. She had to call. She had to. But she didn't want to. She felt weighed down with dread.

She'd been lying here trying to figure out what time it was back in Vancouver. They were eight hours behind. So what time was it there? Somehow she was never sure she'd counted right. And then she'd have to start over again. It was a great stalling tactic.

Hi, Dad. Can I speak to Mum? Hi, Mum. I just wanted to ask you . . .

No matter how she rehearsed it, it was a disaster.

Hi, Mum. Remember that old recorder of yours?

She could ask Aunt Sally about the time difference, just to make sure. But no. It was going to be hard enough to make the call when nobody was around. The old phone was wired into the wall, and she couldn't just pick it up and plug it into a jack inside her room for privacy. She didn't want Aunt Sally to overhear.

Three-thirty here. Seven-thirty in the morning there. Right?

Hi, Mum. You'll never guess what I found the other day. . . .

Seven-thirty. Would they be awake? Hardly likely. Mum liked her sleep on weekends, and this was a vacation. She'd be like a tiger if the ringing phone woke her up.

It was going to be hard enough. *What if she just won't talk? What if she gets mad and denies everything?*

Was there any way of not telling? Could she stumble through the next two weeks, get on that plane alone, smile at them when they met her at the Vancouver airport, and say nothing? Nothing at all?

No. Too much has happened. I'm too different, I know too much.

A soft knock on the door startled her.

"Holly?" It was Aunt Sally's voice. "Frederick and I are just going to pop down to the village for a few things. D'you fancy an outing?"

Heart pounding, Holly jumped up and opened the door. Aunt Sally stood there, purse slung over one shoulder.

"Uh . . . no, thanks. I'll stay." Her breath came in short gasps. Before she had time to think too much, she took the leap. "Aunt Sally—it's eight hours' time difference between here and my parents, right?"

Aunt Sally frowned. "Yes, I think so. You want to give them a ring, do you?"

"Yes . . . if it's okay, that is."

"'Course it is, love. Go right ahead. And we'll not be long. Anything you want from the shops?"

Holly shook her head, dazed.

"Right then, see you later." Aunt Sally bustled down the hall and out the back door.

Holly was left standing in the doorway of her room. *No excuses now.*

SHE SAT in the dim front hall with the rumpled piece of paper spread out across her knees. Slowly, she dialed the number on the ancient black phone. It took forever.

Ring, ring . . .

A trickle of ice slithered down her spine. This was it.

"Hello?" It was Mum. Holly froze. She'd expected Dad to answer first.

"Mum? Hi, it's Holly."

"Holly! How are you?"

"Uh, fine. . . ."

"Is something wrong, darling? It's so early."

"Yes—well, no. . . . Mum, I have to talk to you. I've got something really important to tell you. You're going to think I'm nuts, but just listen for a minute."

"Okay. . . ." The voice was cautious, uneasy.

She took a huge breath, as if for a dive into deep water. "Mum—I found the recorder you dropped in the barn all those years ago."

"The what?"

"The recorder."

"Recorder?"

"And I know what happened. At least, I'm pretty sure I know. You heard the music. Well, I heard the music too. I heard the music when I was playing. The door opened for me, and I went in, and I found the pots. And I accidentally broke the first pot, and . . . Well, I'll tell you all about that later. But the important thing is, the pots are all gone now, and there's no more magic there anymore."

Silence.

"Mum? Are you still there?"

"Holly, you're talking nonsense, absolute nonsense."

"Maybe I am, but then whose recorder was that I found in the barn? The ivory-coloured one?"

"My grandfather had one like that. . . ."

"Aunt Sally says you played it too. And she showed me a picture of you with your flute at your recital."

Silence.

Holly's stomach knotted, but she kept on. "Mum, you don't have to say anything now. I just want you to know that whatever made you run away from here is over. It's finished with. I bet if you played your flute right now you wouldn't hear any echoes."

"I couldn't. . . ."

"I know you couldn't play your flute right now because you don't have it."

Silence.

"Mum . . . where is it? Did you throw it into the ocean? Did you chuck it off the Burrard Street Bridge?"

"Lion's Gate. . . ." A choked whisper.

Aha! "Right by Stanley Park. Very peaceful."

Silence.

"Mum, I'm not trying to trap you. I just have to say one thing: you don't have to hide any of this anymore. It's all over."

"Holly, I—"

"Mum, let me tell you what I think. I think that this is why

157

you've been against me playing music. It just reminded you of what you gave up, and it made you crazy. And I know a bit about what that's like because one day I decided I'd never go back to the pot room, and I tried to practise in the house, and the music came anyway. I couldn't get away from it. And I bet you couldn't get away from it either, not even in Vancouver."

"No. . . ."

"It's over now, Mum. The magic is gone."

Silence. Then after a long moment she heard a rustle, as if the phone were changing hands.

"Mum? Mum?"

"Holly?" It was Dad's voice, edged with fear.

"Hi, Dad."

"Holly, are you okay? Mum looks like you just beaned her with a crowbar. What's happened?"

She gulped. *How much do I tell him? Do I let her tell him instead?*

"I'm fine, Dad. Everything's fine. But I've had . . . some adventures. Probably not the kind you had in mind."

"What do you mean, Piper? Tell me!"

"Dad, you're going to think I'm crazy, but there were these pots in a room in the barn here, and they made music when I played, and they called out to me, and . . . well, I think they called out to Mum too, years and years ago, and she got scared and ran away." She paused, gasping for breath.

"Hold it. What do you mean, 'called out to you'?"

"They were singing . . . and when I broke them, well—I had adventures. But, Dad, that's not really the important part. The thing is, I think Mum heard the music too, long ago, before she left England, before she met you."

"I don't get what you're driving at, Holly. What's that got to do with—"

"Did you know that Mum was a musician before she met you?"

"A—no, what do you mean?"

"She played the flute. Um . . . I don't know, maybe I've said too much already. She should tell you herself." Her stomach was in knots now, remembering how silently Mum had passed the phone over, without saying a word, without saying good-bye.

A long pause. "She . . . she never told me anything about that," he said.

"It's true, Dad. But ask her yourself."

Another long pause. "Holly, I think we both need some time to process this. How about we call you back tomorrow?"

"Sure. Sure, that's a good idea. And Dad . . . ?"

"Yes, Piper?"

"I love you—both of you. Tell Mum I love her, please. . . ."

"I will." His voice was husky.

Tears welled in her eyes. "Talk to you tomorrow," she whispered.

"Bye, darling."

Holly hung up the receiver and buried her face in her arms and sobbed. She missed them so much. She wanted more than anything to be in that far-away room with them, but no. Whatever she had done, it was out of her hands now. Her sobs echoed through the empty house.

THAT NIGHT she lay in bed for hours, watching the moon-shadows glide across the wall in a slow dance. The fatigue of two tense nights and days all packed into less than twenty-four hours weighed heavily on her and yet kept her as tense as a watchful cat.

Could Avartha have been saved? Should I have stopped the Celts?

Was telling Mum the right thing to do? Will she hate me for telling Dad her big secret? I should have kept my mouth shut!

And this last thought always brought the burning tears, the sobs that had to be muffled in the down quilt.

Until at last the tears swept her away into sleep, into dreams . . .

Into a dream where she was running through that black and white landscape of broken mountains, running after someone: a woman, a girl. Long black hair like a flag, flowing blue dress beating like wings around her. . . .

"Avartha! Stop! Wait!" Holly called out again and again. "Avartha!"

At last the racing figure turned, and it was Mum's face that stared back at her, a face full of fear.

"Mum! Stop!"

But she didn't stop, just kept running, running, until the mountains dipped away and they were both running through the darkness of ancient cedars, through the shadows, then out, out into sunlight and onto a narrow sliver of a bridge with cables soaring to the sky.

"Mum! No!"

The figure didn't stop, only paused a moment at the edge before flinging herself into the air, arms spread like wings, blue dress singing as she sailed down, circling like a gull and landing gently on the water.

Holly leaped after her, found her own arms had become wings. She landed beside her.

"Mum!" she said, reaching out.

The face that turned to her was Avartha's, black hair fanning out around her shoulders like a veil. Her dark eyes found Holly's, reproaching her.

"You betrayed me," she said.

"Avartha! Let me explain! I had no choice!"

As she reached out to grab Avartha's arm, it disintegrated into a cloud of black feathers. Holly plunged forward into the cold water, breathed it in, felt herself drowning. . . .

She sat up gasping, choking. She gulped in air, the air of her room. Her heart was pounding. Had she called out? She looked around her at the familiar shadows. She listened. No anxious footsteps, only the soft ticking of the clock in the hall and the sighing of the wind outside. A change in the weather.

She lay down again, shaking, trying to disentangle herself from the dream.

You betrayed me.

It was far into the night before sleep came again.

CHAPTER THIRTEEN
ARCHAEOLOGY

SLEEP WAS A WARM TIDAL POOL. EACH TIME she surfaced, the pounding of rain on the windows pulled her under again. But at last she smelled coffee and rolled over. She glanced at the clock. Almost ten. Had Mum and Dad called yet? She did the math in her head. No. It was still the middle of the night over there. They probably wouldn't be calling for hours.

The lingering dread of the dream still clung to her. Suddenly, Holly sat up knowing what she had to do. She had to get back to Stonehenge.

Into the bathroom for a quick shower, then back to her room to dress quickly. She pulled a sweatshirt over her head, ran a comb through her hair, and bounded out the door.

Aunt Sally was at the sink, washing dishes.

Holly sat down at her place at the table. There was still some toast in the rack and a big box of cornflakes on the table. "Aunt Sally . . . how long would it take to walk from here to Stonehenge?"

"About forty-five minutes, I should think. But there's a bus, you know." Aunt Sally turned to her, surprised. "Matter of fact, I have to pop into the village later, around noon. I could leave you off at the bus station then."

"I—I think I'd rather walk," Holly said, buttering her cold toast.

Aunt Sally gave her a long, measuring look. "You might wait for another day, love. It's foul weather for a walk."

"I know, but I've got my rain jacket and boots." Holly stopped herself. *Careful! She'll think this is too weird!*

"Well, if you're that determined, you must dress warmly. The winds up there can be fierce. And the footpath along the road is a bit treacherous in parts, with all the traffic there along the A303. Frederick could show you the old way, past the Abbey in the village, but I daresay you'd be happier taking the bus." Aunt Sally smiled her crooked smile.

"Hmm," said Holly, mouth full of toast and jam. Frederick. *Do I want Frederick along?*

She poured herself a big bowl of cornflakes and thought about that. Actually, it would be good to have Frederick along. But the less Aunt Sally knew about that, the better.

She mustn't suspect a thing!

"Maybe I will take the bus," she said.

"I've a copy of the schedule here somewhere," said Aunt Sally, rifling through a mound of papers in a drawer. "Here we are." She pulled out a brochure and handed it to Holly.

"Thanks," she said, munching thoughtfully on her third slice of toast.

"I've some hoovering to do first, love, but if you don't mind waiting a bit . . ."

"Actually," said Holly, wiping jam from her fingers, "I think I'll walk into the village myself to get the bus. That's not very far."

"Suit yourself, love. Just behind that little café we were in the other day is where the buses stop." Aunt Sally bustled off down the hall, and Holly soon heard the roar of the vacuum cleaner.

She grabbed the bus schedule and dashed to her room for her rain gear. *The sooner I'm out of here the better!*

Five minutes later she was leaning against the old Morris Minor, talking to Frederick. To Frederick! *Two days can change everything!* she realized. But two days ago was ancient history.

The garage was as much a different world as Avartha's. The shelves were stuffed with tools and pieces of metal she couldn't hope to identify. There seemed to be a dozen cars or pieces of cars hunched in various corners. The place smelled of oil and rust and dust. Frederick had just emerged from underneath the one car that seemed mostly together. He was scowling at her. That was almost a relief, somehow. At least the scowl was familiar.

"I know it's pouring rain," she said. "But I just have to go out there, and I want to walk because . . . well, I can't really explain why. But I don't know the way. Your mum thinks I'm taking the bus. Alone."

"Hmmph," said Frederick. "Bus makes more sense in this filthy weather."

"Look, if you don't want to come with me, fine. Just give me directions from Amesbury and I'll walk out there on my own."

"Hang on, hang on. I'll come," muttered Frederick, wiping his greasy hands on a cloth. "Wouldn't mind going back there myself. But why this minute?"

Holly shivered. "I'm not sure. . . . I had an awful dream last night. I just have to go back there, that's all."

"Right then, give me a moment to wash up."

"Thanks, Frederick. Thanks so much." She smiled at him and watched some of the annoyance drain out of his face.

"What about Mum, then? What'll she say if she sees the pair of us trotting off somewhere?"

"When I came out she was vacuuming the back bedroom. But why don't I go on ahead and you follow?"

"Right. I'll catch you up, then."

Ten minutes later they were walking down the Amesbury road in their rain gear. Frederick clumped along in huge black rubber boots. "The Wellington Boot, Foundation of English Culture," he said with mock solemnity, pointing.

The rain was teaming down, blowing in their faces. *Why am I doing this?* Holly wondered over and over. They trudged on through the village until the road divided.

"This way takes us through West Amesbury, past the old Abbey," said Frederick above the wet swish of traffic beside them.

Holly nodded, not daring to say much. At least he wasn't grumbling and complaining. It truly was an awful day to be walking anywhere.

They passed the abbey, which was now a nursing home, and crossed a small bridge.

"The River Avon," muttered Frederick. "Usually a sleepy little stream down here."

The water was swollen, pock-marked with the driving rain. "Looks like it's having nightmares today," muttered Holly.

Finally the village was behind them and wet fields fell away on either side. The road ended and merged with a busier one. They passed through a pedestrian underpass and emerged on the other side into the noise of traffic.

"Here's where the footpath carries on," shouted Frederick, pointing. "Sometimes it's only wide enough for one, sometimes disappears altogether. Y'awright?"

"Yes, I'm fine," said Holly, swiping a hand across her wet face.

"Right then. Best follow behind me."

She followed him gratefully, trying to shut out the din and the spray of cars beside them and think only of the Stonehenge that used to be. She tried to fit this landscape with that other empty one across which she had walked and run, but she couldn't. Everything had changed.

By the time they came within sight of Stonehenge the pelting rain had eased, to be replaced instead by a fine grey mist. They panted up the last slope along a narrow chalk path rimmed by half-drowned wild poppies. Frederick stopped and turned.

At least he's not scowling now, Holly told herself as she caught up. Just what she needed—something else to feel guilty about.

"You want to pay and go in, then?" he asked.

"I guess so. I hadn't really thought that far."

Frederick's next words were drowned out by the roar of two tour buses leaving the parking lot. She glanced over and saw that there were hardly any cars there this time. She gazed across the road to the monument. Only a few stragglers.

"Yeah, let's go in," she said. "Looks like we might be between tours." She rummaged in her pockets for coins and found instead the sharp sliver of pottery.

"Here, let me," said Frederick, clomping ahead of her to the wicket to buy tickets.

They hurried through the dark underpass that ran under the road and puffed up the path on the other side. There were only four or five other tourists, most of them huddled beneath umbrellas.

Holly halted at the low rope barrier that separated the monument from the path. She gazed up at the stones. Gusts of wind blew the mist into her eyes.

"Amazing, isn't it," breathed Frederick. "To think we were

over there, just yesterday, with all them wild men with swords and such. Doesn't seem real, does it?"

"No." Holly stared at the middle of the stone circle, where she had stood at the centre of power, and tried to imagine it all again. The veil of light streaming out from her, the high, sweet music all around. And Korak's voice.

She drew out the piece of pottery and gripped it fiercely.

"I brought this, just in case it might—I don't know—do something here . . . something magical," she said, then shook her head in annoyance, embarrassed. "Stupid! Stupid, I know. . . ."

"Never mind. Brought mine too." Frederick sheepishly pulled his shard from an inner pocket.

They exchanged uneasy smiles.

Holly took a deep breath. "Frederick, thank you for coming all the way out here with me in the pouring rain. And—and thank you for coming into the past that last time. It would be really hard to come back here, with everything that happened, and not be able to talk to anybody about it—to somebody who was really there."

He looked down at the soggy path, kicked at it with his boot. "Like I said, it was a real adventure."

"Do you think your mum bought my story about falling off the swing? She had me cornered there. I had to think up something in a hurry."

Frederick shrugged. "Dunno. She seemed to."

Holly sighed. "It's so hard to keep all these secrets. Especially since . . . since I talked to Mum yesterday."

"You rang them?"

"Yeah." Holly kicked the gravel at her feet.

"And you weren't wrong about her, then?"

"No. No, I guessed right. But Mum . . . I don't know, it wasn't the greatest conversation." She stared at the wet pillars,

167

eyes blurring with rain and tears. But she fought the tears back and gritted her teeth.

"It's not just Mum. I just can't shake the feeling that I let them down," she nodded towards the monument, "that I let Avartha down. If I could only know for sure that everything worked out, that they managed to live happily somehow, that Avartha learned to love Camanom, that Serak found somebody else, that Evaken became a great sorcerer like Borekarek."

"Hang on a minute," he said, turning. "You *saved* them, don't forget that. You saved their lives! You said so yourself."

"Yeah, I guess. . . ."

The wind spattered a few big drops of rain on her face and into her eyes. She rubbed them, and when she looked again, something had changed. A dense mist was settling in around them. She could see nothing but the stones ahead and Frederick beside her. Holly rubbed the splinter of pottery between her fingers as she suddenly heard laughter.

She stared at the centre of the ruined horseshoe and blinked. Misty shapes were moving there, turning in wide, slow circles. The shapes grew clearer, and their voices rang out from the fog—a low chuckle, the guffaws of young men, and the musical laughter of a woman. They were dancing. Bearhead and wolf-head whirled around a black-haired woman and a man with a ponytail.

"Avartha!" Holly called out.

But the mist enveloped them, and the outlines of heads and arms and cloaks blurred. The laughter faded until all she could hear was the *whush, whush* of the wind. The fog had swallowed them.

"Frederick, did you see?"

"Something . . . something like shadows."

Right behind her Holly heard a low chuckle. She spun around.

It was one of the tourists she'd seen, an old man with a battered wool hat pulled down low over his face. But his eyes—Holly knew those eyes, hard and sparkling like stars.

"Korak!"

He winked at her, and with one quick step was at her side. He laid a skeletal hand on her arm.

"Well done, Maregi!" hissed the ageless voice.

Holly shook her head. "No, no, not well done at all."

He chuckled again. "Maregi, your task was never to change what is but to help them accept what must be. Tell me, now, what did you see here in my enchanted mist?"

Holly gazed at the stones. The fog was already thinning. "I think . . . I think I saw them dancing . . . dancing together."

"And what did you hear?"

"Laughter."

"Quite right. As I have said, well done, Maregi."

And with a flap of glossy wings, he was gone, a raven now, soaring above the ruined pillar-stones. The mist had melted away. There was only the rain.

"Who was that bloke?" asked Frederick, frowning, as if waking from a dream. "Couldn't quite make out what he was saying. He bothering you?"

"No," said Holly, trying to follow the path of the raven's flight with her eyes. "No, he wasn't bothering me. He had something important to say. Come on, let's go."

She started back along the path towards the entrance with Frederick clomping along behind her.

"Hang on!" he sputtered. "What did he say, then? Who was he?"

"Korak."

"What, the old codger with the prophecy?"

"Yes." She stopped in the dim shelter of the underpass and

turned. "He . . . well, you saw something inside the stone circle, didn't you?"

He scratched his head. "I did see something, and then you
shouted."

"Well, it was them: Avartha and Evaken and Camanom
and Borekarek. They were dancing and laughing."

"Dancing . . . well, that's good then, isn't it?"

"Yeah." She turned away, unsure.

They emerged from the underpass on the other side of the
road. Holly turned back to gaze at Stonehenge one last time.
Then she looked eastward. Suddenly, she ran to the edge of the
parking lot to where the fields of stunted grass dipped away
and miniature daisies shivered in the wind. She stepped once
more onto the damp green land, perhaps the land she had run
across in the moonlight that night.

"Oy!" shouted Frederick behind her. "Look, will you?
Here's the bus—let's catch this one back to town!"

Holly turned reluctantly, then noticed that the rain was
pelting down again. "Okay," she said, walking towards him.

The bus was almost empty. Holly rubbed at the misty windows, but it didn't help much. Raindrops snaked back across
the glass, obscuring everything but the blur of green fields as
they lurched along the road.

She sighed. Why didn't she feel any better?

"What's the matter, then?" said Frederick, squirming
beside her. "You said they were laughing. Happy. That's what
you wanted, isn't it?"

"I guess . . . I guess it wasn't really about Avartha and
Stonehenge after all," she said slowly. "My dream, I mean . . ."

Frederick snorted. "I don't hold much with dreams. Never
make any sense."

"This one didn't really, either."

You betrayed me.

Avartha's eyes, but whose voice? Mum's?

Mum's. And what was the betrayal? Letting the big secret slip to Dad yesterday? No, more than that. Her own love of music, every note she had played, every moment spent with Dad practising—it had all been a betrayal of Mum's hopes for her, hopes for a life free of that knife's-edge desire for the joy that music brings.

"If it weren't really about Stonehenge, then, I'll wager it was about your Mum. My crazy Aunt Gillian, as I've always called her—strictly to myself, that is."

Holly winced, then sighed. "Yeah, I guess it really was about her . . . and about me."

Frederick coughed and stared out the window. "If you take my advice—which you needn't do, mind you—but if you take my advice, you'll give it up and let her solve her own problems. She is a grown-up, after all. Savin' a rag-tag bunch of prehistoric folk is enough work for one person. You can't go round the world savin' everybody."

The bus slowed and pulled into a bus loop.

"Now then," Frederick continued, "we're back in Amesbury. Fancy a hot cup o' tea?"

"Sure."

She followed him off the bus in a daze. The rain had stopped, and a few shafts of sunlight were slanting through the clouds as they walked through the village. Just opposite the library stood a whitewashed house festooned with pink balloons. A sign on the wall said "Amesbury Museum," but this was overshadowed by a huge banner that proclaimed, GRAND OPENING! FREE ADMISSION! Several people dressed in old-fashioned clothing hovered at the doorway, smiling at visitors.

"This must be the museum your mum was talking about," said Holly, pointing. "Want to go in for a minute?"

"A bit gaudy, isn't it?" muttered Frederick under his breath.

"True," agreed Holly. "But at least we don't have to pay to get in." She led the way, trying to

ignore the silly man in an outrageous costume with puffy green sleeves who greeted them.

"Trying to look like old Will Shakespeare," mumbled Frederick as they ducked inside.

Three steps led downward to the main floor of the house. The room was filled with glass display cases lit from within. Holly and Frederick moved to the first case at the far left.

The museum seemed to contain objects from all periods. There were Victorian gowns and an array of eighteenth-century guns. Holly realized that as they moved to the right they moved backwards in time. There were rusted medieval swords, and a cluster of pale aqua glass bottles from Roman times.

She forced herself to look at the next display. The room seemed to spin suddenly, and she grabbed Frederick's arm to steady herself.

The case held the contents of a local Iron Age grave. A black-and-white photograph of the excavation showed a skeleton lying on its side, knees curled up. But it was the objects below the picture and commentary that made her heart skip a beat. Beside a golden Celtic-style torque and two gold bracelets lay a fragment of dirty brown fabric. Pinned to one corner of the cloth was a silver brooch. A raven brooch.

"Frederick!" she gasped, unable to do anything but point at the brooch.

"Isn't that the one Avartha had on?"

"Yes! I gave it to her! I bought it at the Salisbury market!"

"Then—then this is her!"

"Yes!"

Holly stared at each object in the case. There was a large clay pot and some other items of jewellery—several pins decorated with animal heads and a variety of pale blue and green glass beads.

Then she clapped a hand over her mouth. In the bottom right corner, with a cascade of blue beads spilling over its edges, was her flute case.

"Although found in the grave containing Iron Age artifacts as shown, this twentieth-century flute case testifies to some degree of modern grave disturbance," said the terse comment on the little white card beside it.

"Let's get out of here!" whispered Holly.

Frederick nodded, and they turned to weave their way back through the crowd. They reached the door and hurried outside. Holly jogged across the street to the library and leaned against the door.

"She's dead, Frederick!" she moaned.

"'Course she's dead. She's been dead a couple thousand years."

She glared at him.

"Sorry!" He reddened. "But it's true. You got to see that."

"I know," Holly groaned. "It seems impossible, though, when I was with her only . . . only yesterday. And then, just now at Stonehenge, I saw her dancing, heard her laugh again."

"I know."

"But . . . the brooch and the flute case . . . they were there! Buried with her, like they were important to her."

"That's obvious, isn't it? Which means she didn't hold nothing against you for what happened. She remembered you as a friend, all her life."

"You think so? I guess that's true, isn't it?'

"'Course it's true."

Holly stood silent for a long time, watching the people passing on the street with unseeing eyes.

Finally she heard a chuckle beside her. Frederick was leaning against the library wall beside her, arms crossed, grinning.

"Worth a laugh, though, isn't it—this grave here?" He jerked his head towards the museum. "All these big archaeologists trying to figure out how a flute case got in with all that old stuff! Cor! I'd a loved to see their faces!"

Holly imagined those puzzled faces, and she started to laugh. She laughed and laughed until she collapsed against the wall beside Frederick. She laughed as if some spring coiled tightly inside her had snapped. They were both still laughing when Aunt Sally roared up beside them in her car.

"'Allo!" she called, leaning across the passenger seat to the open window. A wave of astonishment washed across her face as she gazed from one to the other. "I was about to drive up to Stonehenge after you, Holly! Your parents just rang. They've booked a flight to London. Day after tomorrow. Thought you'd like to know right away."

"They're . . . they're coming here? *Both of them?*"

"That's what Gillian said, yes. I must say she's taken me by surprise with all this. That must have been some chat the two of you had yesterday!"

Holly leaned anxiously against the car window, suddenly cold all over. "How . . . how did she sound? Did she sound . . . okay?"

"Yes. Very tired but fine. Now mind you don't go reading too much into that, love. But," Aunt Sally smiled, "I've a feeling it's a good sign, them coming over here."

"They're coming! That's fantastic!"

"Hop in, now, you two. I can't stop here forever. Why don't we all have a nice cup o' tea down the street?"

"We were just about to do that when I got distracted," Holly said as she climbed into the back seat.

"And perhaps now you can tell me what's *really* been going on," Aunt Sally added with a smirk at Frederick, who had just climbed in beside her. "I thought you'd be underneath the Morris this morning, young man. Not tramping round town with the dreaded Canadian cousin."

Holly saw him blush as they pulled into traffic, and she groaned inwardly. *Now we have to come up with another excuse!* But the knowledge that Mum and Dad were coming—coming here *together*—warmed her and made it hard to worry about anything.

I faced down two armies ready to kill each other. Surely I can manage one cheerful aunt!

She took a deep breath. "I realized I really did want to walk all the way to Stonehenge," she said. "So I asked Frederick if he'd come and show me the way, and he did."

Frederick cleared his throat. "No harm in being friendly for a change, eh Mum?"

Aunt Sally grinned over at him. "Well done, Frederick. Very nice of you."

Jagged patches of blue sky had opened up overhead. The street was bathed in golden light as Holly followed Aunt Sally and Frederick into the Raven's Nest Café. As she caught the door, she heard the flap of wings overhead.

She gazed up into the rain-washed air, and smiled.

Historical Note

ALTHOUGH THIS STORY is based on what little we know about early Britain, some elements are a matter of speculation. A confrontation between local people and Celtic invaders like the one described in this book would be seen as unlikely by many archaeologists, who insist that there is no real evidence that Stonehenge was in use as a ceremonial site after 1100 BCE—five hundred years before this story takes place. This means no bones, weapons or pottery in nearby burials date back to the time when the Celts were beginning to arrive from Europe. On the other hand, bones and rusted swords never tell the whole story.